# The Derbyshire Set ~ Book 1

## Regency Historical Romance

Second Edition ~ Revised and Expanded!

# The Earls Unexpected Bride

# Arietta Richmond

**Dreamstone Publishing © 2016 - 2023**

**www.dreamstonepublishing.com**

Second Edition 10 May 2016, updated April 2023

Enhanced and Expanded.



ISBN-13: 978-1-925165-98-2

# Disclaimer

This is a work of fiction. Names, characters, places, organisations, events, and incidents are either products of the author's imagination or used fictitiously.

ARIETTA RICHMOND

# Dedication

For everyone who had the grace to be patient (and with this particular book, you've been very, very patient!) while this book, and every other book that I have written, was coming into existence, who provided cups of tea, and food, when the writing would not let me go, and endured countless times being asked for opinions.

For the readers who inspire me to continue writing, by buying my books! Especially for those of you who have taken the time to email me, or to leave reviews, and tell me what you love about my books, and what you'd like to see more of – thank you – I'm listening. I hope that you enjoy this new series (which features some appearances by old favourite characters from the His Majesty's Hounds series), just as much as my other books.

For my growing team of beta readers and advance reviewers – it's thanks to you that others can enjoy these books in the best presentation possible!

And for all the writers of Regency Historical Romance, whose books I read, who inspired me to write in this fascinating period.

# Books by Arietta Richmond

## His Majesty's Hounds

Claiming the Heart of a Duke

Giving a Heart of Lace

Enchanting the Duke

Finding the Duke's Heir

Healing Lord Barton

Loving the Bitter Baron

Rescuing the Countess

Attracting the Spymaster

Intriguing the Viscount

Being Lady Harriet's Hero

Redeeming the Marquess

Winning the Merchant Earl

Kissing the Duke of Hearts

Falling for the Earl

Betting on a Lady's Heart

Courting a Spinster for Christmas

Restoring the Earl's Honour

A Scandalous Spring (An additional short story)

The Scent of First Love (an additional short story)

From Soldier Spy to Lord (contains the first three books in one volume)

To Love a Determined Lady (Contains Books 4, 5 and 6 in one volume)

Love Heals a Lord (Contains Books 7, 8 and 9 in one volume)

To Love a Dashing Lord (Contains Books 10, 11, 12, and 13 in one volume)

For a Lady's Honour (Contains Books 14, 15, 16, and 17 in one volume)

## A Duke's Daughters – The Elbury Bouquet

A Spinster for a Spy (Lily)

A Bluestocking for a Baron (Rose)

A Minx for a Merchant (Primrose)

A Maiden for a Marquess (Iris)

A Vixen for a Viscount (Hyacinth)

A Diamond for a Duke (Camellia)

An Enchantress for an Earl (Violet)

A Heart for an Heir (Thorne)

## The Family Sagas Collections

The Barrington Saga

The Morton Saga

The Dartworth Saga

The Edgeworth Saga

The Windemere Saga

The Chester Saga

## The Nettlefold Chronicles

The Duke and the Spinster

A Duke in Autumn

To Wed an Earl

To Dance with the Dangerous Duke

A Christmas Bride for the Duke

The Marquess Elopes

The Scandalous Countess

## Lady Canterford's Conspirators (The Mayfair Ladies Poetry Society)

A six book series (coming soon)

## The Duke of Traithewood's Legacy

The Marquess Marries a Twin

## The Regency Gothic Series

Lord of the Storm

Lord of the Darkness

Lord of the Shadows

Lord of the Lost

## The Regency Scandals Series

The Gift of a Christmas Scandal

Lady Mariel's Scandalous Love

Christmas with *That* Duke

Lord of Dragons (written with Kyrii Rayne)

## The Derbyshire Set

A Gift of Love (Prequel short story)  A Devil's Bargain (Prequel short story - coming soon)

The Earl's Unexpected Bride

The Captain's Compromised Heiress

The Viscount's Unsuitable Affair

The Count's Impetuous Seduction

The Rake's Unlikely Redemption

The Marquess' Scandalous Mistress

The Marchioness' Second Chance

A Viscount's Reluctant Passion

Lady Theodora's Christmas Wish

A Remembered Face (Bonus short story – coming soon)

The Duke's Improper Love (coming soon)  A Gentleman's Unconventional Courtship (coming soon)

The Derbyshire Set, Omnibus Edition, Volume 1 (the first three books in one volume.)

The Derbyshire Set, Omnibus Edition, Volume 2 (the second three books in one volume.)

The Derbyshire Set, Omnibus Edition, Volume 3 (the third three books in one volume.)

## Themed Collections

The Regency Christmas Hearts Collection  The Regency Christmas Love Collection

The Regency Spring and Valentine's Hearts Collection

The Regency Summer Hearts Collection  The Regency Autumn Hearts Collection

The Regency Spring Love Collection  The Regency Summer Love collection

## The 'Her Duke' Collection

Her Summer Duke

Her Passionate Duke

Her Absent Duke

Her Determined Duke

Her Generous Duke

Her Christmas Duke

## Other Books

The Scottish Governess

The Duke's Christmas Vow

Lady Augusta's Letters

The Crew of the Seadragon's Soul Series, (coming soon - a set of 10 linked novels)

# Table of Contents

ARIETTA RICHMOND

# Chapter One

As the water closed over her head, the events of the last few minutes replayed themselves in Catherine's mind, with the intense clarity that sometimes comes in dreams. But this was all too horribly real.

The water was such a cold shock after the warm sun of the bright May morning, and part of her believed that she would drown, even while she flailed against it.

~~~~~

She had been walking along the road from Lavenham to Harteston, returning from a visit to her mother's friend, Mrs Brown, when she first heard the sound of a horse's hooves.
~~~~~

Not those of just any horse she might have heard, picking its steady way along the hard-packed earth of the road, but a powerful, fast horse, obviously in some considerable hurry, hooves pounding out the urgency of its pace. It stopped her right in her tracks for a moment, so out of place was that rush on this quiet road. The thudding rhythm, the pounding of its progress - she heard it coming up ahead of her, on the other side of the bridge, although she could not yet see it, for the trees and the high bank on the side of the road quite obscured what might lie around the corner.

She was, for no sensible reason, filled with a sudden dread - not a horrible sense of fear, or a real worry for her safety, but a dread nonetheless, at what was approaching, at the source of that clamour, coming towards her from around the corner. Then, taking her first few steps onto the bridge over the Shimpling stream, she saw him.

He came clattering onto the wooden slats of the bridge, apparently unconcerned by the prospect of any passer-by. The first thing that struck her, in that first instant that she saw him, was the rider, his thighs, to be precise, inappropriate as that may be. He sat the horse with the confidence of long years riding, and controlled the stallion without apparent effort. His powerful thighs, flexing as they held him effortlessly in place, spoke eloquently of power and authority.

She was embarrassed by her thoughts, and a flush of colour came to her cheeks, but she could not drag her eyes away. His breeches, creamy white and tight as skin, clung to him, giving definition to every muscle and sinew. His boots were almost as magnificent, well-worn black leather, the same colour as the horse's glistening hide. Everything about him spoke of wealth and power.

He sat atop his animal with an easy grace, casual almost in his manner, unencumbered by a glove or a hat. From the other end of the bridge, she could take in all of his magnificence, the broad strong chest, the shoulders that seemed to span the entire width of the road, the chin that jutted forward. His face was strong, robust, and masculine, with chiselled cheek-bones below dark eyes.

And on top of it all, above the square manliness of his face, and the rather wild look of his eyes, was a rich mane of dark hair, shot through with red and gold tones, that glinted in the sun, tousled, swept aside by the onrushing wind and lent buoyancy by an irrepressible energy that could be felt the moment you saw him. She suspected that hair was not easily controlled. So focussed was she on the sight in front of her, that she had simply stopped walking, unaware that she had done so.

The horse did not stop as it came towards her. Its rider seemed not to see the small and simply dressed young woman on the bridge, who also had cause to cross the green expanse of the Shimpling stream, late this Thursday afternoon in May.

He spurred his mount on, charging over the rickety structure, as if he were master of all he surveyed.

She realised, with a gasp, that he was not going to stop for her, and, with a cry, threw herself to the side. Almost brushing the stallion's flank, she hurled herself against the side rail, but could not stop herself from toppling, tumbling over the rickety rail and into the stream.

With an almighty splash, and a roaring in her ears, she was in the water. She could feel the slimy grasp of the reeds, feel the weight of all the water on top of her as she flailed about.

She panicked.

She had never learned to swim. The mill pond at the back of her village school had always seemed too terrifying to enter, and she had never learned. The thoughts rushed through her mind, replaying, over and over, the last few minutes, as she desperately fought the water, all to no effect.

She grasped around for the bank, for something to cling onto, but nothing presented itself to her flailing hands. She could barely see in all the darkness of the stream, and could feel her dress and petticoats soaking up the water, weighing her down, pulling her to the rocky bed of the stream. Every moment she became more certain that she was about to drown.

But then she felt something, a firm hand, a grasp from above, a man's grip. She was dragged up until she broke the surface of the water, spluttering uncontrollably. Some heroic force hauled her onto the river bank, onto the dry grass just above the shore. She was held in a standing position, only by the strength of her saviour's grip – he legs as yet refused to support her.

She looked up, still panting for breath. It was him. Of course it was him. Her assailant had become her saviour. He held her close, waiting to see if she could stand, if she would pull away.

Looking past his shoulder, she could see that the stallion was tied to a tree in the background, pawing at the grass, obviously wishing to be away and running again. She looked up into those dark devilish eyes and could not help but smile, even though her teeth chattered from the chill of the water.

"Are you quite all right?" he asked, with an uncertainty to his voice that betrayed his concern.

"Yes, yes quite all right."

Her voice was shaky, and she was still short of breath, nerves still jangling from her watery encounter.

She suspected, strongly, that she sounded unconvincing. Her eyes met his and she drank him in – he was just as good to look upon close up, as he had been from a distance.

"I must thank you kind sir, by your hand I appear to have been rescued from a watery grave."

"It was only because of me that you found yourself in such a predicament to begin with" he said, without hesitation.

His tone was that of man used to making declarations, to ordering the world around him. She realised that he held her slight frame in his embrace still, and could not but feel a shiver at the sensation. She knew that she should pull away, should put distance between them, that this was highly inappropriate, yet she did not want to. It was pleasant, every once in a while to have a saviour this handsome.

She was not used to anyone else taking care of her, except her mother.

"I must apologise for my haste in crossing the bridge," he continued.

"It appears to have compromised your passage somewhat. I was, unfortunately, rather distracted – after a trying morning, I just wanted to ride, and ignore the world."

"Oh, not at all sir," she replied, (although it was patently obvious that he spoke the truth). She was still shaky, and unable to find anything sensible to say - she had often struggled to maintain her composure around handsome gentlemen – in fact, she had very little experience with gentlemen at all. Regardless of the fact that he had caused her fall into the stream, her gratitude to him for saving her was immense, for surely, without him, she would have drowned.

"Please!" he cried, cutting her off. "Do not deny it, the fault was entirely mine."

He released her, apparently having finally noticed that they were in a rather inappropriate proximity to each other, and stepped back cautiously, watching to make sure that she could stand on her own. His immaculately tailored coat of bottle green superfine clung to his shoulders, quite as beautifully tailored as those breeches, and showing of his devastatingly well-made body. She was horrified to see that the fabric was marred by splashes of water, and that the pristine whiteness of his breeches had rather suffered from the muddiness of the stream. Yet she was shocked to realise that she felt a desire to be back in the embrace of those arms, it had made her feel safe, to be held so, and she could not but consider what might follow such an embrace.

Her breath hitched at the thought, and, as he looked at her, patiently waiting to see what she would do, his eyes still full of concern, she became conscious of her wetness, of how it must make her face red and shiny, of how her hair was clinging unflatteringly to the side of her head and of how her bodice was clinging rather revealingly to her body, the cloth made somewhat translucent by the water. The light stays that she wore, and the somewhat old and thin state of the fabric of her gown, did little to conceal her figure, once totally soaked in the water of the stream. It brought a blush to her cheeks, but he did not look concerned.

"I must regretfully confess, I can often become rather distracted when I take my afternoon ride."

As he spoke was looking over at the horse, gesturing.

She looked down, blushing, and ashamed of her state, and realised that he was wet up to his knees, his beautiful Hessians undoubtedly ruined.

He had waded into the stream to save her, compromised his own dignity for her safety - how remarkably unlike most of the noble gentlemen that she had met before (admittedly, there were not many). This, she allowed herself to think, was quite an unusual man.

That, she thought, following the line of his hand to the horse, was quite some animal. It would take a remarkable man to tame it.

She could not ride – a humble village girl had no chance or reason to learn – her feet, or the innkeepers cart, had always been enough for her. Yet she knew a quality horse when she saw one.

"I recently acquired this splendid mount" he waved to the horse once more "at an auction at Tattersalls. I was informed by my dealer, Mr. Redgrave, that he was bred in the stables of the Maharajah of Nackulpande, renowned as the greatest horse breeder in all of His Majesty's colonies".

He fixed his gaze back on her. "His studs are renowned for their power and virility. Thaddeus here came at a not inconsiderable expense, but I believe such extravagance to have been worthwhile."

She nodded, unfamiliar with such matters – she could tell that the horse was quality, but of what type, or to what extent, she had no idea. She had never once ridden a horse herself.

"He is as powerful as he is headstrong. I see plenty of my own self in him – That is probably why we suit."

He looked back, when she made no response. She could think of nothing to say, she was too caught up in watching him, in the obvious energy that he brought to everything he did. It was compelling, and exciting.

He mistook her silence for disinterest.

"I pray I have not bored you with all of this discussion of the stallion. As an unmarried man, I am not often called upon to converse with ladies outside the confines of the drawing room and the ballroom. But where are my manners – here I am rambling on about my horse, and you are standing there, dripping wet and cold. Come, let me help you up the bank to the road."

He offered his hand. She clasped it, and felt a quaking in her breast, a quivering in the bottom of her stomach. He was unmarried! And so handsome and wealthy! How was it even possible? This chance encounter appeared to offer one of the great excitements of her life, and she could already feel her mind brimming with new passions, new hopes, new desires. Village girls dreamed of things like this, of accidental meetings with handsome, wealthy noblemen, and, of course, those dreams always had a happy ending, with the couple falling in love. She shook herself, mentally – this was reality, no dream, and the chances of anything happening were remote, to say the least.

"I thank you sir" she said, a little shakily, as she reached the top of the bank, and stepped on to the edge of the road. "And I must say that it is not at all tiresome to hear so eloquent an insight, on a subject with which I was not previously familiar."

"You flatter me" he said, with an ironic smile. "But I know enough of young ladies to have some awareness that the subject of stallions and auction houses does not generally greatly excite their interest."

He smiled and she could not help herself but smile warmly back. He had revealed another side, the tiniest hint of softness, of charm.

"Tell me miss, what is your name?" he enquired, with a renewed gravity.

His warmth was hidden again, tantalising her in the background. She examined her feet humbly before she could look him once more in the eyes.

"My name is Catherine Thornberry."

"A charming name. The sweetness in the wilderness. I have always had a fondness for it." She blushed at this spontaneously poetic response. "Allow me to introduce myself; I am Charles Rockingham, Earl of Stanningfield. I must confess that I am surprised to have stumbled upon you. I had presumed myself to be familiar with every pretty young lady in the county, but it appears that at least one had slipped my notice - and barely a mile from my own estate. Amusing is it not, how these things can pass us by?"

"Oh yes sir, indeed it is!"

She spoke in a rush, excited by his flattery. The Earl of Stanningfield, here on Shimpling bridge, plucking her, Miss Catherine Thornberry, from the stream as if it were the most natural thing on earth! Catherine had a horrible suspicion that she was gushing, that she was making a fool of herself, but this man had an odd effect on her - she found that she struggled to think sensibly in his presence.

She was awestruck. Having never seen the Earl before, but having heard, from her friends and from her mother, much of his exploits, she had not anticipated that he should be so young, so handsome, so gallant in his readiness to help a young lady in distress.

The tales she had heard painted him as a rake, as a man with a great deal of life experience.

She had expected an older man, heavy of body from overindulgence, and jaded in his attitude to life. Nothing could be further from the man who stood before her. She tried, as hard as she could, not to allow another red blush to flush her face, but it was all too much. It was all unreal, as if in a dream.

"Do not look so thunder-struck Miss Thornberry." He spoke forcefully. "You may have formed some idea of my reputation on the basis of idle parish gossip, but I must assure you that the overwhelming bulk of it is hearsay."

"I'm sure that it is sir, undoubtedly!"

She was gushing again - it had always been a profound concern of hers that she came across as too enthusiastic in the presence of gentlemen. She checked herself.

"I have been at great pains to impress upon the county my courteous nature, but regrettably, I have an unfortunate past that seems to stalk me like a wolf." She nodded gravely. She had heard some such stories, and always suspected that there might be some truth to them. Nevertheless, being of a kind and trusting nature, she had always wanted to believe that they were false, or at least, misrepresented. She found that she did not want to believe this man capable of terrible things. "We shall speak no more of such unpleasantness. Please, allow me to escort you homeward. It would be the least kindness I could offer after our unfortunate interaction on the bridge."

"Oh sir, that will not be necessary. I am quite capable of completing my journey unaccompanied."

"I insist," he said, not as a politeness, but a declaration. "You are shaking like a willow in a gale and as wet as a hunting dog, and all on my account. It would be most improper of me to abandon you here." His expression was serious as he spoke, and, again, she felt that the concern in his eyes was genuine. "I will not have it said of me that I abandoned a fair and defenceless lady, drenched, on the side of the road. And besides" he added, with a glimmer in the corner of his rich brown eyes "what on earth would your neighbours say if I did?" They shared a chuckle at his little joke. "Thaddeus awaits!"

Laughing, he took her hand, tugging her towards the horse.

"But sir!" Catherine exclaimed "I regret to confess, I have never ridden before, and I do not know how!"

"Good heavens above!" he seemed genuinely shocked "Not ridden a horse? Why it is one of life's greatest pleasures! I would not wish to deny the thrill of a good, vigorous ride to my worst enemy. Allow me..." before Catherine even had time to make an objection, he had scooped her up. She clasped his thick, muscular shoulders and found suddenly that her face was close to his, so close, in fact, that she could see every bristling hair, every tendon in his neck. Close inspection did him justice. His scent came to her, an earthy mixture of horse, leather, and an undertone of some more exotic scent, some cologne of citrus and spices. It was like nothing she had smelled before. She found it stimulating, and extremely pleasant. "Time I think, for your first ride!"

He laughed, before depositing her unceremoniously to sit sideways across Thaddeus' saddle. She felt the animal shifting beneath her, full of vigorous life. She clung to the abundant mane that drifted back over her hands, holding on as if for dear life, anxious that the horse might suddenly take off without warning, or that it would deposit her once again into the stream. It had a will of its own and a powerful body after all, but her saviour, the Earl, held firmly to its reins. He gently stroked the horse's nose to calm it, putting it under his spell, before firmly commanding it to stand.

Then in a single, graceful movement, he swung up into the saddle, lifting her to sit, still sideways, across his knees, his arms either side of her shaking body, and took charge of his stallion.

"Hold on tight," he declared, and she obeyed willingly. There was a moment where she hesitated, aware that her soaking clothes were already shedding even more water onto his attire, before a movement of the horse convinced her that she was quite happy to sacrifice his clothing for her safety. She wrapped her white arms, still cold and wet, about his splendid torso, as tightly as she dared, her head resting against his shoulder. The shape and definition of his firm abdominal muscles could be made out beneath his coat and shirt. The sensation quite took her breath away. "Now where would you like me to take you, Miss Thornberry?" he asked, after a moment.

"To Hawthorn Cottage in Harteston," she replied. "Do you know it?"

"I know Harteston, but not the exact location of Hawthorn Cottage. A fine village indeed - do you live there alone?"

As he spoke, without warning her, he had shifted Thaddeus into motion, and already they were crossing the bridge at a gentle canter. She was, again, impressed at his gallantry, as he was now heading the opposite way to his own original route.

With the unfamiliar rocking motion of the horse, and the stress of its forward motion pressing her ever more tightly against the body of her saviour, she could feel something thrilling stirring within her. A new sensation, pleasurable, dangerous, was creeping up her inner thighs and into her bosom. She bit the back of her lip. It was entirely inappropriate for her to be thinking such thoughts about this man.

He was far above her, he was courteous enough to have saved her from drowning, and here she was thinking like a wanton. Well, she thought that's what it was – actually, she had no idea, no idea beyond the fact that her body was reacting to its proximity to his – and she was scandalously enjoying it.

"Or…" he continued with a roguish chuckle, "have you a sweetheart in Harteston perhaps?"

This time she was wise to him. This time she played the game.

"I am unmarried, my Lord. However…" she added, with a slight laugh of her own "I must confess that the innkeeper's son and I have developed something of a rapport in recent times. He is a most handsome young man."

"Oh undeniably," replied the Earl, rising to her challenge. "Indeed, I have often thought to myself, on visiting that very fine inn, that he would make a most attractive catch for a young girl in the village. Nevertheless," He paused in his speech a moment, as if considering the right words to use. Thaddeus was picking up speed. Her lower body was assailed with a new vigour, rocked against the Earl's thighs, and the front of his body, in a rather intimate fashion. The warmth of his body was penetrating the chill of her wet clothes – it made her want to press herself even closer against him. Having obviously chosen his words carefully, he continued, "Are his manners and breeding not a little coarse, for a young lady of distinction, such as yourself?"

Catherine did not allow herself to laugh, but she was overwhelmed. This man was clever. He knew the workings of the female heart. Moreover, by asking this question, which she now, perforce, had to answer, he had coaxed a difficult admission out of her, concerning their relative status.

"I am but a humble schoolmistress, sir," she said reluctantly. "I have education and, I flatter myself, a little breeding – but certainly not any significant status in the world."

"Stuff! I could tell the moment that I saw you, that here is a lady who carries herself well, evident poverty notwithstanding."

"You are, indeed, courteous, my Lord. Nevertheless, I could never make any claims to be a noble lady. My mother, with whom I share Hawthorn Cottage, has long maintained that we are descended from the de Quincy family, who came over with William the Conqueror no less, but I fear, from what little she is willing to tell me of the detail, that lineage may be rather obscure now, to say the least."

"The de Quincys?" he came back, not bothering to disguise how impressed he was. "Not bad at all. Tell me, how does a girl with such a fine pedigree find herself reciting the alphabet to ungrateful village brats?"

"I suppose some ancestor of ours must have fallen on hard times," she said, keeping her poise. Thaddeus was going at quite a speed now, and it was necessary to raise her voice. She tried as hard as she dared to disguise the quaking in her body that the movement of the ride, and the sensation of his body against hers, was giving her. "Mother has mentioned a gambler, in my great grandmother's generation, who may have lost us our estates. That is long ago, and of no relevance to our lives now. I am unused to luxury, and the life of a humble schoolmistress is easy enough to bear."

He had exposed a quiet sadness in her, a longing. For years she had ignored her mother's pining after their heritage, her obsession with the importance of ancestors on their family tree, but now, in the presence of a real gentleman, she was, for the first time, embarrassed by her circumstances.

She had no land, no money, no prospects of a higher match. All she had ever hoped for was to make an honest living and to marry one of the boys in the village, but now, something else had stirred in her, passion, ambition, a reaching for something more. Thaddeus' movement seemed to fill her with a greater lust for more in life, as well as most interesting sensations in her body, with every galloping stride.

"I suppose someone's got to force some knowledge into 'em," he laughed, urging the horse along. The countryside sped by. She took in long, drooping willows, plump cows chomping in the fields, water mills churning, as they had for hundreds of years. It was not such bad country, Suffolk, especially as it had such charming people in it. The speed at which the road went by amazed her, so used was she to the time it took to walk this distance. "Still, it is a terrible shame for a great and noble family to have fallen on hard times. Alright, I suppose, if you're happy enough looking after other people's infants, and cavorting with innkeepers' sons, then I can think of worse fates."

"Why yes sir. I suppose I am happy enough."

She knew, even as the words came out, that she was lying to him. Had someone asked her the question yesterday, then that answer would have been truthful, but today, she was alarmed to discover, something in her had changed. She was no longer satisfied with what she had.

"Well, jolly good then."

He appeared to focus his concentration on riding now, for the first time taking his attention away from her. She could not help but feel a small pang of disappointment.

Thaddeus thundered on, down a shallow hill, and then splashed across a ford.

Before she knew it, having never ridden upon a horse or experienced just quite how fast these noble animals could move, she was in the village of Harteston, shaken by the journey, quivering and awake deep in her body, and intensely aware of his body where it pressed against her.

"Here we are" he declared confidently. "Harteston - where I suppose I shall leave you."

"Yes. I must thank you my Lord, your kindness has saved me much effort, and possibly even preserved my life. For surely, had I not drowned, by now I would have taken a terrible chill on the road home."

"No need to thank me Miss Catherine, I am sure that you would have done the same were our roles to be reversed."

"I suppose I would have. Thank you again."

She released her grip on his body, regretfully, and he lifted her gently, supporting her as she slid down the side of the horse to land on her feet.

She hesitated, unsure of what to do now, part of her not wishing this moment to end, but unable to see any reason for it to continue. Then, not wishing to betray the feelings that he had stirred in her, and holding her crumpled bonnet high upon her head, she dipped him a curtsey, and set off for home.

The Earl however, had never been the kind to let a pretty young lady get away from him, so coldly and suddenly. As she had silently, privately hoped, he swung out of his saddle and came straight after her, catching her in just a few steps. Grasping her fragile waist, he turned her suddenly towards him. She gasped, her eyes wide open. He pulled her against him, and the heat of his body against hers felt like fire rushing through her veins.

"Not so fast," he whispered, close against her ear. "We haven't even said a proper goodbye," and then, just like that, he kissed her, fully, without apology, on the lips. He gripped her for a moment that felt like it should last forever, a moment deserving of a painting or a symphony to capture it and preserve it. She felt his strong tongue, his hot mouth, and his firm lips. Their bodies pressed together, seeming moulded just for that, and she could sense the longing they shared could feel the hardness of his desire, tangible through their damp clothing. Her body throbbed, with the sensation of the kiss, and the vitality imparted by the ride.

Just as suddenly as he had captured her, he pulled back, looking a little shocked himself, at what he had just done. He mumbled goodbye, and swung back into the saddle, heading for home.

Catherine stood a moment, dazed, watching him go. She had never felt such a thrill in all of her twenty-four years on God's earth.

# Chapter Two

Charles Rockingham, Earl of Stanningfield, was bemused. He rather feared that he had just made a fool of himself, in front of a young lady.

Not something that he had ever been prone to doing.

*That is,* an insidious thought reminded him, *except for the colossal fool he had made of himself, at 17, with Monique.*

He pushed the thought aside.

That was old history, beyond being changed. Today, he should be focussing on his current problems. And what problems.

He groaned as it all forced itself back to the surface of his mind, now that he no longer had a ready distraction to hand.

He chose to shove the thoughts away again, an act made easy by the fact that his clothes were uncomfortably damp, and his toes squished alarmingly in his boots, which were, he suspected, full of water.

They were certainly coated in mud.

The condition of his attire would draw the wrath of his valet, and he expected that Johnson would be effective at making his disapproval known, without ever saying a word.

Still, even if he had rather made a fool of himself, it was, he decided, worth it. He had been in such a temper when he had left the house. His morning, reading through applications for the role of Theodora's Governess, had been enough to drive anyone to despair.

They were, universally, terrible. The sort of women he would definitely never want in his house – the sort who would turn a bright, if sometimes difficult, girl into a prudish, boring society Miss, incapable of conversing on any topic except the weather.

He knew that the best solution to such a mood was a good hard ride, on a quality horse. And Thaddeus was quite the best horse that he had ever owned. But it had been spectacularly unwise of him to ride, at that pace, along the road – over the fields would have been a far better choice.

Well too late to change anything now.

And…. Would he want to?

The girl was beautiful – and, it seemed, completely unaware of that fact. He had not seen her, not until it was too late. He had been so wrapped in his thoughts that the world around him had been barely registering.

He might not have seen her, but the thump against his leg as he rode across the bridge, followed by the scream, and the huge splash, had certainly attracted his attention.

At that point he had no idea who or what he had just caused to fall into the Shimpling Stream, beyond the fact that it was almost certainly a person, as nothing else screamed quite like that.

Unwilling to leave anyone floundering due to his inattention, he had hauled Thaddeus around (somewhat against the stallions wishes at the time!) and gone back to investigate.

What he dragged from the water was a delectable surprise.

A girl, or young woman rather, her shape thoroughly displayed by the unfortunate saturation of her gown, her piercing blue eyes shocking in her pale, water-soaked face, her sodden hair seemingly a golden brown colour – although the mud made it hard to tell. She had blushed charmingly as he held her, waiting for her to be steady on her feet again.

She held herself well – there was obviously some breeding there, or at least some education, but the gown was, as far as he could tell after its dip in the stream, rather worn. It had been good quality once, but the hems showed signs of it having been turned, and the fabric was thin from wear.

Thinness he deeply appreciated, as it ensured that the water had made it almost translucent. It had taken all his concentration to avoid staring at her breasts rather than her face.

Apart from the sodden gown, and its exposure of her attractions, there was something about her that took his breath away, in that first look.

It took only a moment to realise what – her shape, the turn of her cheek, the fall of her hair, even sodden, brought to mind, just for a second, Monique.

He had pushed that recognition away, and focussed on her more mundane attractions.

He had been a rake for too many years not to appreciate a woman's body when he was given an unexpected viewing.

But, it seemed he was rather out of practice.

The sight of her body had robbed him of sensible, coherent conversation, and he had made a complete ass of himself, prattling on at her about the horse, of all things. Women, in his experience, did not give a damn about horses, so long as they transported them where they wanted to go. He was depressingly sure that he could not have made a bigger fool of himself if he had tried.

And then, to top it off, he had taken her home. What else could a gentleman do? He certainly couldn't leave her to walk four miles in a soddenly transparent dress, when she was already shivering from the cold! What if she had met some oaf along the way, who thought to take advantage of her? *Like you wanted to,* said that insidious voice in his thoughts. She was schoolmistress at the parish school – the school that his family funded, had funded for 50 years now, for the good of their tenants and the villagers. A less suitable woman for him to find tempting he couldn't imagine.

The feel of her body against him, of her arms around him and her soft breasts pressed against his chest, rubbing against him with the movement of the horse, the feel of her rounded derriere, rubbing against his thighs, pressing against his manhood, had been enough to drive a saint wild.

The wet fabric of her gown was no barrier, and the water soon transferred to his breeches as well. They might as well have been skin to skin, he could feel the detail of her body so clearly.

His cock had hardened in response, making the ride an exquisite agony. She must be an innocent, for she had appeared to genuinely not notice, even though Thaddeus' every stride had thrust the evidence of his arousal against her nether regions.

Which made his behaviour at the end of the ride all the more despicable.

Not only had he flirted with her, in a rather suggestively inappropriate way, but he had, at the end, kissed her….

Hard…. Full on the lips.

He had not intended to, but, when she turned away, all stiff and unsure, after that ever so wobbly curtsey, and simply began to walk off, her ridiculously crushed and sodden bonnet perched on her equally sodden hair, he had not been able to stop himself – he wanted a reaction, wanted more than just a departure.

He did not know why - he was, obviously, simply a fool. But he had gone after her, grabbed her and pulled her to him. In the middle of the damned village street, for pity's sake! And she had tasted divine. Her innocent response had been to press into the kiss, and the feel of her body fitting so perfectly against his had roused his passion like no woman had for years. Had the chiming of the town clock not interrupted, he might almost have taken her there, on the street.

He was, most definitely, a fool.

And, he was no further ahead with solving the governess problem.

He was just as frustrated by that as before, but now, he was frustrated in an entirely different way, and sodden as well. He sighed, and steeled himself for Johnson's response to his maltreatment of his attire.

# Chapter Three

"Well of course there's not a single chance he'll marry you."

"Mother!"

"Don't speak out of turn child! I know gentlemen and their ways. He just wants to use you, as he uses that horse you seem to be so very taken with."

"But I'd never ridden before."

"No you had not, and quite right too – you've no need of riding and horses – where would you go? And considering what I've heard about the Earl's predilections, you would have been better off nowhere near riding with him!"

Catherine's mother paused for a moment, to stir the copper pot that was perched above the fire.

They would eat the same type of food as they ate every night- a mealy stew with perhaps a little bacon or fatty pork, supplemented by some vegetables grown in their garden and some bread. An old weaving of the de Quincey family tree might hang above the fireplace, upon the blackened brickwork, but that was history, and now, in the present, they could not afford to dine on anything more extravagant than this.

"I may be old, but I know gentlemen," her mother continued, repeating herself as she often did lately. "A fellow like him's nothing more than a cad, a bounder. He sniffs out a pretty young girl who may be of noble heritage, but is poor and unimportant, as far as he is concerned, and he thinks only to have his way with her."

"Mother!"

"I only speak the truth, Cathy dear. I only have your best interests at heart. No good will come of this, I tell you."

Catherine thought to reply, but she could not muster the courage. Deep-down, she knew that her mother might be right. Her mother's words were giving voice to a fear that she herself had felt, ever since the Earl first plucked her out of the stream. Maybe he was a bad man. Maybe all the rumours one heard about him were true.

"He did at least have the decency to stop and save me," she said at last, in a reedy voice that sounded a little desperate, a fact that annoyed her, even as she spoke. "You must at least concede that that was an act of considerable kindness?"

"Oh yes, of course," her mother replied, in a voice with a tone perilously close to a whine. "I suppose yes, he was good enough not to just let you drown, after it was by his actions that you were deposited into the Shimpling stream in the first place. Yes, I suppose the fact that he's not actively a murderer is one small positive we can mark down in the ledger."

"Oh mother, I wish you wouldn't use that tone!"

"What tone?"

"That sarcastic, bitter tone you always like to use, whenever we speak about young gentlemen. It's almost as if… as if you don't even want me to fall in love and get married! As if you want to talk me out of leading my own life and keep me here by the hearth with you forever, supping at stew and getting old by myself!"

"Now, now!" her mother replied, suddenly kinder. "Why on Earth would make you an assumption like that about your own dear mother, eh?" She had come over, and placed her arm around Catherine's shoulder. Unlike the Earl's, Mother Thornberry's arms were thin and frail. Catherine could feel them, all skin and bone wrapped in a scratchy shawl. It was a comfort to have her mother's embrace there, but not always a warming one. She worried at how thin her mother seemed to be getting – she was not, when Catherine added it up, really very old at all, so it must be the result of their poverty, of eating so little, over so many years. It distressed her to realise that she could not do more for her mother, who had done so much for her. "All I'm saying" her mother said, softly, "is that a young lady like you has to be careful. You don't want to end up embroiled in some short-lived affair that strips you of your honour, but leaves you with nothing, save perhaps, an illegitimate child. Take it from me…"

She stared now into the middle distance, out of the little window of their cottage, towards the far fields, her expression sad and longing.

There was pain and sadness in her voice, pain that came from hard-won experience. Catherine knew. She had grown up knowing. Her mother had made this very same mistake herself.

Catherine herself was the illegitimate issue of a sudden affair, carried on beneath a haystack. She knew little more of it than that, as her mother always refused to speak of it further, beyond the warning for Catherine not to be foolish enough to repeat her mother's errors in life. She wished that she did know more, that there was some way to ease the sadness that her mother had carried for so many years.

"Men can be wonderful of course. Handsome, dashing, strong and charming, all at once, as if they are the most perfect creatures in all of creation. But they can also be brutes. Something stirs within them, some spirit, or instinct and all they can think about is a woman's body, her femininity. They have no care for a woman's feelings, or her life beyond the moment when she satisfies their desires."

"Mother, I am aware of the simple biology of it all."

"Are you child? Are you? I have tried to teach you more than is considered proper for a young lady to know, to protect you, and, as a result, I fear that you do believe that you know, but take it from me, you don't. I don't think you entirely understand the risks that you run in becoming involved with a man. I certainly didn't at your age."

"Then what would you have me do mother?" Catherine had risen from her chair by the fireside, throwing off her mother's embrace, and was standing now on her own feet, the very same feet that had, earlier that day, dangled down the side of The Earl's prize stallion, while her body was pressed so arousingly against his. Turing to face her mother, she asked the question that had kept her mind in turmoil ever since she had arrived home.

"What should I do?"

Her question, asked imploringly, drew a wry smile from her mother's lips. The little wrinkles around her eyes tightened and she seemed to be forming new wisdom behind her eyes, even as Catherine watched, hoping against hope that there was an easy answer to an impossible question.

"You must be clever Cathy, that is all." The words were a long time coming, and Catherine had begun to wonder if her mother would answer her at all.. "You must anticipate what the Earl will do, and act accordingly. Bear in mind, at all times, that he lusts after you, and formulate a strategy on that basis. Consider also…" and she turned around to point straight at the family tree. The illustration was beautiful, with the de Quincey coat of arms - a rampant Panther with a crown around its neck – surmounting the detailed listing of those who were her forebears. Frustratingly, the illustration had been created more than eighty years ago, and the link between herself, and her mother, and those listed on it, was not at all clear to Catherine. "…that yours is amongst the highest heritages in all the land. The blood of Jocelyn de Quincey, and his noble ancestors, flows in your veins. We may not have money, titles or estates, but we do have that, and can never be stripped of it. If you can remind the Earl of that, he will be impressed by you, and may consider you a possible match. It all falls to you now, my Cathy, only you can revive the fortunes of our once great family. Don't squander this one chance."

Catherine looked up at the coat of arms. It was a proud image, but had been battered by time and obscurity, faded on the page. Her heart swelled with the thought of it, the possibilities that her mother's words brought to mind, but she trembled at the pressure that those same words placed on her. Could she do it?

Could she really find herself married to the Earl of Stanningfield?

"I believe in you, Catherine Thornberry," her mother said, gravely. "But don't you go making any foolish mistakes. You're still only a girl, after all."

She was still only a girl, a maid even. It was true, her mother was right, even if she didn't like to admit it. She had to be clever, and careful, but her heart sang for him, for that kiss they had shared on the outskirts of the village.

With the thought of that, she was filled with a new warmth. Oh, it was all so exciting! She felt young and pretty and on the cusp of a great love affair! In her mind, she already thought of him as Charles, however lacking in propriety such forwardness might be, and the desire to see him again ran through her, bringing a flush to her face at the thought.

"Now child," her mother said, "if you are to become the great seducer of the county of Suffolk, I think you'd best keep your strength up. Come and have a bowl of this stew."

The words were spoken lightly, with a true sense of humour in them, yet they were underlain with an aching desire for what might come. Catherine smiled, sat down willingly, and ate her fill.

Charles handed Thaddeus to his groom, and took himself into the house through the servant's door, in an attempt to minimise the spread of mud. That was a failure.

Wilton eyed him expressively as he made his way up the stairs, and Johnson greeted him in silence, with an expression of outright horror on his face. A hot bath was called for, his maltreated clothing and boots were stripped away, and he was left to soak in silence. If only his thoughts were as silent and peaceful as the room around him.

He was in turmoil – he did not know what to do about any of his current problems.

For the last three years he had been, comparatively, respectably behaved.

He had taken no new mistress, and had kept those short affairs that he indulged in to a strictly business basis – and exchange of the satisfaction of physical needs, with nothing emotional, and nothing exposed to the critical eyes of the *ton*. It had been a most considerable change from his previous approach to life.

Three years of 'good behaviour' had not completely dispelled the rumour and gossip that his previous life had generated, but it was fading. He could hope that, in time, they would forget. He had chosen to change, not for himself, but for Theodora's sake. From the day that she had been delivered into his care, at the age of eleven, he had vowed to provide her the love and care that her mother was no longer there to provide. For the sake of her reputation, and eventual acceptance by the *ton*, when she reached a suitable age for her come-out, he had pushed aside many of his own desires, and to his mother's delight, begun to behave 'as an Earl should'. It had not been easy at first, but had become more so with time.

He had, six months ago, when old Mrs Walsh died, finally acquiesced to his mother's wishes, and agreed to make the long-standing agreement between the families formal, with his betrothal to Lady Blanchette Cavendish. He did not love her, but, in the ranks of the ton, love between husband and wife was rare - marriages were for dynastic reasons, nothing more.

He knew that he needed an heir, and that Theodora needed another woman to help her grow up, now that Mrs Walsh was gone. He had hoped that Lady Blanchette might be that woman. It was, it seemed, a vain hope, for Theodora had taken her in strong dislike, and, in her strong willed way, made that abundantly clear. But by then, it was too late – the betrothal had been made public, and it was his duty to go through with it.

Lady Blanchette had been rather a surprise – whilst she was rather cold and harsh on the surface at times, she had proven to have a hidden core of passion. Once they were betrothed, their parents had seen no harm in allowing them a walk in the grounds, some time alone together – time which had resulted in a passionate kiss, which he had begun in exploration of what he might live with for the rest of his life, and which she had taken further, with a response that had taken his breath, and all of his control, away.

After more than two years of minimal physical release, and that with women who were as jaded as he had become, Lady Blanchette's relatively innocent passion had been too much to handle – he had, to his later regret, pulled her into a nearby outbuilding, and taken her there, with little care for her experience – a fact of which he was still somewhat ashamed.

She had seemed somewhat shocked by his demanding and forceful actions, but she had responded with some strength of passion as well. He had found her confusing then, and did still, to this day. He excused his actions to himself, only by the fact that they were to marry. She had, since that time, once more given him her body, for reasons that he could not determine, but otherwise she had been rather haughty, and not always pleasant. He wondered if she lacked confidence, and acted this way to appear stronger than she was, or if she was simply of mercurial temperament. If the latter, he was, perhaps, in for a difficult life.

Now, he had a marriage to Blanchette to deal with in a scant month or so's time and the need to find a Governess for Theodora, who might have the strength of mind to manage her, enough education to teach her, and enough gentility in her breeding to know at least some of what Theodora would need to know, to behave appropriately as a young lady of the *ton*.

The marriage arrangements were in his mother's control – a fact which was both a relief, and terrifying. The Governess situation was all his problem, and he had no answer.

But today had tried his patience sorely, and he was now struggling not only with the need to find a Governess, but with the fact that a certain Miss Catherine Thornberry was taking over his thoughts. He could not wipe from his mind the image of her, standing before him on the bank of the Shimpling Stream, saturated, looking more like a water nymph from some erotic fantasy than a respectable young woman. His thoughts became heated as he remembered the press of her body against his, and the delicious pain of his hardened cock being rubbed against her body by every stride of his horse, as he delivered her home. He was hard again now, lying back in his bathtub, just from the memory.

He wanted her.

There was no denying it.

Why her, he wondered, why now, when he was soon to marry, and she was by far too below his station to be marry (even had he been able to), and of by far too respectable a family and position for him to simply use. Not that, he realised, he would wish to do such a thing now. Perhaps in his youth, but no longer. But he wanted her. More, he realised, than he had wanted any woman, since Monique.

It was insane to feel so, yet he did. Resolutely, he tried to push her from his mind again, and focus on solving the Governess problem. The bath water had cooled, but his body had not. He still ached with need – perhaps if he eased that, by his own hand, he could stop thinking of the damn woman, and deal with everything else.

His release came hard, and fast, his mind imagining her beneath him as he came, but his thoughts were no clearer afterwards. He dragged himself out of the tub, and scrubbed himself dry with unnecessary force, then called for Johnson to dress him for dinner. Staring vacantly ahead, ignoring Johnson's still offended attitude, he thought once again about the qualifications he wanted in the Governess.

He was not sure such a woman existed, as most governesses were daughters of the lesser families of the *ton*, fallen on hard times. Few had much education themselves, and even fewer had any idea how to either teach, or command respect – so how could he ever hope that they could deal with Theodora effectively?

Something about that last thought made him pause – there was something there, something that he was missing.

He worried away at it, mentally, as Johnson, poked and prodded, brushed and combed him into his clothes and into a well turned out presentation. Then it came to him, in a flash of inspiration. The answer had been right before him this afternoon, he just had been so distracted by the 'packaging' that he had not realised.

Miss Catherine Thornberry fulfilled all of his requirements in a Governess, exactly. She was quite well educated, she had practice teaching, and getting her students to respect her – the village children were not an easy lot to manage! And she was of at least reasonable breeding, although sunken to poverty. She knew how to curtsey and had at least the minimum of socially acceptable graces. It was inconvenient that she also had the ability to drive him to distraction just at the sight of her figure, but he was sure that he could learn to manage his reactions – Theodora's need for a Governess came first.

He startled out of his thoughts, as Johnson spoke, for what must have been the third time.

"I believe you are ready, my Lord – will that be all? I fear I must return to the… resurrection… of your clothing, if you need nothing more from me now?"

Johnson's tone left his opinion of the treatment of the clothing in no doubt.

"Thank you Johnson, yes, that will be all."

Charles turned, as Johnson left the room, with a pleased smile on his face. He resolved to visit the village tomorrow, and speak to Miss Thornberry, to offer her the role of Governess to Theodora.

Perhaps today was not such a loss after all.

Except for his favourite pair of Hessians.

The next day Catherine could barely focus, at all, on her work at the school.

How on earth could she be expected to?

The curtain was coming up on the great drama of her life and it had all of her energy, all of her attention (internally, she admitted that, perhaps this was melodramatic and overly optimistic, based on one meeting, but that did not stop her feeling that way). In the morning she stumbled her way through basic arithmetic.

The children looked confused, and seemed to be struggling to follow. She would lose track of her thoughts as they came to her, and frequently needed to sit down. Whilst talking them through one particular sum, she started giggling remembering him telling her all about the horse.

One of them asked her:

"Miss, why are you laughing?"

All she could think to say was - "Oh, nothing, it's none of your concern."

After the children had had their lunch, she had become grave and serious, thinking constantly of the consequences and the risks of her affair, should she be able to make it become so, in truth. She tried to tell them about the exploits of Henry VIII but Charles Rockingham filled her thoughts. She even referred to Thomas Cromwell as 'Charles' once, an embarrassing mistake which caused all of the children to laugh.

"Who is Charles Miss?" one of the girls asked in a strong Suffolk accent. "Is he your sweetheart?"

"No, no of course not," she stuttered in reply. "I was merely thinking of Charles I, the king during the Civil War," - she did not sound very convincing. "That was all. I was thinking ahead. We'll be studying him next week."

The girl eyed her suspiciously.

"Do you even have a sweetheart, Miss?"

"Jemimah, you will stop asking improper questions if you know what is good for you!"

Catherine found a tiny reserve of strength and managed to implement some discipline. Jemimah Blenkinsop however, would not be silent.

"You're pretty enough to have a sweetheart Miss!" she declared. "All of the young fellows in the county should be asking for your hand!"

"Well that is very kind of you to say, young mistress Jemimah," Catherine replied, blushing. "But please, if we could concentrate our attention on history for the present time, we are here for you to receive education, not to indulge in girlish gossip."

Despite her best efforts though, it was no use. She could not focus at all on teaching the children, her mind was on Charles, on his robust strong face, his broad, broad shoulders, his muscled thighs, his devilish wry smile, and of course, that kiss. The kiss that they had shared already felt like the most significant moment in all of her life. She desperately wanted another, a chance to find out what more might happen, if such a kiss continued.

Later in the afternoon, shortly before the children were to be released for the day, Catherine was just directing their attention towards the practice of writing, and spelling, when she heard a tap at the window. Surprised, she turned to face it, and was both shocked and delighted in equal measure, to see that it was the Earl himself, this time in a splendid jacket of rich dark crimson, as beautifully tailored as his coat of green, holding a riding crop and grinning through the grimy window pane.

What a sight!

She gasped in astonishment, and was filled at once with questions, anxieties, warmth, and longing. He was here! How on earth could he be here, what was he doing? It was so improper, for an earl to lower himself to come to the village school like this, interrupting her working day, so sudden, so (she dared to hope...) romantic! Or was something wrong?

Still, he was smiling, waving at her to come out and greet him.

The children stared at the window, clearly confused at the sight of this unfamiliar and well-dressed man beckoning their schoolmistress so unexpectedly. It could never have made any sense to them she thought, if she had tried to explain her reaction, and truly there was nothing she could say to explain his presence. The power of her feelings and the dark beauty of that man waiting for her, made her shake with nervousness as she turned towards the door.

This was an unusual school, the result of the charity of the Earl's family, and some other local nobility, and of the enterprise of the local vicar – who, unlike many 'so called' churchmen, actually cared for his flock, and believed that even girls should be educated. The donations of the nobility, plus the fees paid by the families who could afford to contribute, were just enough to pay Catherine's wages, and to buy some supplies for her to teach with. She was dedicated to her work, and genuinely cared that the children should have a chance to learn, no matter what their status in life.

"I'm terribly sorry children," she improvised "I'm afraid I should have given you prior warning. That gentleman is here on urgent parish business. I shall have to speak with him, I shouldn't be more than a few moments. In the meantime…" she was already halfway to the door, rushing towards what she hoped would be the Earl's powerful embrace, "finish your exercises on the slates."

Without a moment's further hesitation, she burst outside to greet him. He had moved away from the window, and was standing with his legs wide apart, tapping the riding crop against his brown leather gloves. He was taller than she remembered, and even more magnificently attired. Next to the deep red of his coat, the unblemished cream of his breeches, the glint of the richly polished leather of his boots and the perfectly executed cravat that topped it all off, she felt perfectly plain in her simple grey-blue dress and petticoats. She wished, suddenly, that she had had more time to think about what she would wear today, wished that she had money for a maid, whose opinion she could consult, who could curl her hair and advise her on the angles that best suited her face. Charles outshone her this afternoon, indeed he would probably have outshone all of Suffolk, and beyond. She had never seen a man this handsome in her entire life.

"I hope I'm not disrupting the children's studies," he said, his lip curving slightly at the edge, into a half smile. "I wouldn't want the parish to be turning out dullards after all."

"Oh no, not at all!" she spluttered unthinkingly.

She was filled with a desire to move into his arms, to kiss him wildly, but she knew that this would be beyond improper. She blushed at her own thoughts. Apart from being improper, it would most definitely be liable to startle him and show her feelings, too suddenly, all at once. Besides, the children might see, or worse the vicar... This planning to seduce the man into wanting her was somewhat more complicated a thing than it had seemed, when she was talking to her mother!

"What were you teaching the children?"

"Just a little writing and spelling, nothing too taxing or important."

"Writing and Spelling is quite enough. I was forced to learning grammar too - I could never stand the subject myself, awfully dry," he said, casting his thoughts back to his school days with an enchanting grin. "But then, I never was much of a scholar really — my tutors despaired of me. I was always too interested in riding and hunting."

He gestured vaguely towards an old oak tree, to which he had tied Thaddeus.

The memory of that invigorating ride came to Catherine, and she could feel the same stirring in her loins, hot and damp, a strange aching in her lower body, the like of which she had not felt before yesterday.

Yesterday, surely it was longer ago than that, since these over-powering feelings had first come to her?

She felt as if she ached for this man for a lifetime, as if it had always been her destiny to unlock the secrets of womanhood, and of men.

Her eyes met his and they held each other's gaze. She had piercing blue eyes and knew that they were one of her better features. She let him notice them.

"Girls too, for that matter," he finally said, unconsciously wetting his lips with his tongue, as if a little embarrassed to admit it. She knew enough to know what that meant. "Girls always interested me a damn-sight more than any book ever could."

"Reading can be a most pleasurable pastime," her words were innocent, but made him think of reading the sort of books that young ladies most definitely should not read. Turning away from his intense gaze, she continued, "If you take the time, and find a good subject, or an author who interests you."

"Is that so?" he asked straight away, playfully.

"Tell me Miss Thornberry, if you had to select an author to recommend, to an unscholarly gentleman such as myself, little versed in the art of letters, whom would you call to my attention?"

"If I had to select just the one," she replied whimsically "I should say Mr. Henry Fielding. His novels possess a certain energy, and an easy humour that I believe you would find to be compatible with your own…" she looked him up and down, his casual gait, his long well-formed legs. She wet the edge of her lip, in a movement that he found more sensuous than Catherine could ever know, "… distinct personality."

"Very well," he said. "I shall endeavour to track down a volume of his, if what you say is an accurate reflection of my character."

He stroked the cleft in his chin as he spoke.

"I am sorry if I am speaking out of turn my Lord," she said, newly serious, "but I presume that you did not ride out all the way to Harteston, and interrupt the academic formation of my charges, merely to discuss with me the pleasures of English literature."

"No indeed, I fear you have worked me out, Miss Thornberry, I had other business with you."

"Then what pray, brings you here this afternoon? I must remind you that I have a lesson to be getting on with. We have already provided quite enough of a spectacle for the children. I shall not be able to stop them talking about this for weeks."

"Of course, Miss Catherine, forgive me my lack of consideration. I was merely wondering whether, given the great inconvenience that Thaddeus and I inflicted upon you yesterday, and the pleasure, which I presume to be mutual, which I found in your company, if you would consider something of a business proposal from me? I would like to offer you the post of governess to my young niece, who is my ward?"

Catherine was stunned.

This was a most unexpected turn!

An offer of work, at the Earl's estate?

It was strange, and she was immediately confused.

What did he mean by this?

"As governess?"

Her confusion was evident in her voice, and he seemed to see the need to explain, for he went on.

"Yes, as I said, to my young niece, who became my ward a few years ago. Her old Nanny unfortunately passed away not long ago, and she needs company, schooling, and discipline. She is quite an agreeable girl, if a little stubborn at times – she is just fourteen - I believe her age is approximately that of many of your young charges, back there in the schoolhouse. Considering your qualifications in the field of education, your experience with commanding attention and respect from children, and the rapport we both share... I had hoped that you would agree – I believe that it would be of benefit to both of us, as well as to Theodora."

He eyed her appreciatively, but also almost pleadingly.

She blushed and looked away.

Was that his motive?

Coax her up to his house with work and then have his way with her, of an afternoon, after lessons were over?

And would that even be so bad a fate, she dared to think?

The thought intensified her blushes, and she chided herself sharply for showing her feelings on her face.

"…I really do need someone to start almost immediately and I thought you might be willing to take up the post. I've advertised, but I am yet to find anybody else remotely suitable. I could easily match whatever the parish is paying you for schooling its' children, indeed I'd be willing to increase your salary significantly, if that were what it would take to secure your services. What do you say?"

"Oh, my Lord, this is most unexpected!" she exclaimed.

Her head was spinning, questions consumed her.

What should she do?

Abandon her employment for what might be a truly respectable role, or might only be the cover for a strange and illegitimate affair? (Or perhaps it was an affair that would only ever take place in her imagination?)

Or should she turn down what was possibly the chance of a lifetime?

"I am of course, profoundly flattered that you consider me to be qualified to undertake so significant and personal a task as the instruction of your own niece. Only, I must consider my responsibility to the parish, to the children."

"Yes of course, we wouldn't want them to go uneducated, but I am sure that there are plenty of well-qualified young ladies in the county, who would be more than willing to take up such a vacancy, if it were to become available."

That was true enough, she thought. Why only the other day a young woman from Lavenham had come to the schoolhouse, enquiring about the possibility of employment there.

A replacement could certainly be found for her, her duties were not binding.

"There is also the question of my daily journey to your estate. It is some distance from my cottage, and as you are well aware, I do not own a horse or carriage of my own."

"The solution seems to me to be simple enough. I have, at the risk of sounding churlish, plenty of surplus room in my house. You could happily lodge there, if you wouldn't consider the prospect too improper or disruptive. Indeed, I would prefer you close at hand, to deal with whatever dramas Theodora may have, at odd times of night or day. Over the last two years it has become abundantly obvious to me that young ladies can be prone to some drama, which gentlemen are not well equipped to deal with! If your mother were to be in need of company at times, I could quite easily have my Steward, Featherstone, arrange to run you down in my carriage, if the walk were found to be too taxing for a young lady, or the weather were inclement."

He reeled it all off rapidly, as if he had already given this plenty of thought.

Catherine was astounded by the man.

"My Lord, you seem to have considered every possible eventuality! You make it very difficult for me to refuse your generous offer."

"I am a man who knows what he wants," he said, looking her straight in the eye, and raising his eyebrow in a way that made her feel he could look straight into her, and divine her improper thoughts. It was another overpowering moment, echoing the previous day, and she was once more under his spell. "I know also how to go about getting it."

He turned and headed over to the tree where his horse was waiting.

"I would like you to come to Havisham Hall, to see the staff, to meet Theodora, and to allow us to discuss the salary and conditions, before you make a final commitment to the role – which I most heartily hope that you will accept. I shall have Featherstone send the carriage around to collect later this evening, if that would not be disagreeable to you?"

Catherine could barely contain a gasp. It was all happening so suddenly, he was inviting her to his estate already! Yet it was sensible – she wanted to see what situation she would be placing herself in, before she made such a commitment.

"Yes my Lord, if you feel that is necessary, I would be able to make such an appointment."

"Excellent. If you feel that we will come to an agreement, then please, plan to begin tomorrow. You will be returned to Hawthorn Cottage tonight after our discussion, to prepare for tomorrow. I'll see you at five o'clock then. Farewell."

With that, he swung once more into his saddle and with a small wave in her direction, set Thaddeus to a rapid pace out of the village. She wondered, idly, if he ever went anywhere at a more sedate pace.

Catherine was a little saddened not to have shared another kiss with him (impossible as it would have been, in the middle of the village street), but she was amazed at this gesture which seemed to be one of kindness and affection, as well as practicality.

Could it be possible? Was he laying the ground for an affair between the two of them? Or was this simply a position, with nothing more to it?

She could not possibly know, but, later that evening, she would surely come closer to finding out.

Resolving to go along with the situation, to do her best for his niece, but also her best to further a relationship with him, she smiled. She would use all of her womanly wiles (unpractised as they were) to get what it was that she now knew she desperately wanted, more than she'd wanted any single thing before – that being Charles Rockingham, the Earl of Stanningfield himself.

She turned, resetting her expression to the serious one appropriate for a teacher, commanding the blush to fade from her pale, fair face, and went back into the schoolhouse to finish her lesson.

"You should hear some of the things they say about him in the parish," said her mother in a haughty, condemnatory tone, stirring her stew pot idly. This was not the first time that Catherine had heard all of this, and she suspected it would not be the last. "Mrs. Brown says that she once heard from a serving girl, who worked up there on the estate for a couple of years, that he's had mistresses all over the world - France, Holland, Spain, the West Indies, even in India. He's travelled widely so they say, and left a trail of jilted lovers and unwanted children everywhere he's gone!"

"Mother you can't honestly expect me to believe all of that! People will say anything down in the Inn, and in the tea shop, especially if it's about their betters."

"Betters? Better, him? I wouldn't be so sure. He might be of high breeding Cathy my girl, but mark my words – from what I've heard, he's a wrong 'un in other ways – or at least he has been – the things they say he's done! You just be careful now. They aren't Christian some of the things you hear. Why, they say he's got a child he fathered with one of his fallen women, up in that house, living with him! It isn't right at all that sort of thing, most improper. But then, that's typical of the nobility – their wealth lets them live by different rules."

"Mother I'm not interested in this sort of idle chatter. If you are so disapproving of my prospective employer, then why on earth were you encouraging me in this endeavour only yesterday evening?"

"Oh, not disapproving my child, not at all. These are only words of caution which I feel obliged to impart to you, as your dear mother. It would not be very responsible of me, would it, if I were not to share what I have heard from those that have a little knowledge of these things?"

"No mother, I suppose it would not be. But pray, do not torment me so!"

Catherine was nervous.

She could not be anything but nervous, the clock on the mantelpiece was ticking away and every stroke of its hand brought her fate closer.

It was after four o'clock, and the imminent arrival of the Earl's carriage loomed large in her mind.

She could feel a flutter of nervous anticipation, building at the bottom of her stomach, and her mother's gossip was only making it worse.

"He may be your prospective employer," her mother continued "-but I dare say he's prospectively a lot more besides. Keep a close watch on him child, and on yourself. I can see that you're taken with him! No good will come of an affair out of wedlock. You must do it for the family – convince him to marry you, not just use you."

She gestured once more to the coat of arms above the fireplace.

There was so much pride and pressure invested in those symbols of her past. She looked at them and she pictured the knights of the de Quincey family, resplendent in their armour and with the same proud symbols painted on their shields and banner.

There was so much family honour to be lost and won, so many great names to try to be worthy of.

"Now eat your stew and we'll hear no more of it. You must first secure this employment that has been offered, and then take things from there."

Her mother handed her a bowl of stew.

There was a little bacon in this batch, the village butcher must have put his prices down. That probably meant that it was on the turn.

This poverty was all she had ever known, living on cheap stews and lighting their home with tallow wicks rather than the proud, but expensive, wax candles they knew they deserved. She could barely imagine what wealth she might see in the Earl's home.

It frustrated her, that she could not give her mother more, that she seemed trapped in this simple and bare life.

She longed for something greater.

Perhaps that chance would come.

"Oh Mother," she said, with a melancholy tone. "I hope you do not feel that I am abandoning you."

"Not at all child, not at all!" Mother Thornberry replied immediately. "You're all I have in the world, it is true, but I always knew this day would come. You're a pretty young miss and I've done all that I can to bring you up correctly. It's only right that you should go off in pursuit of a husband."

"Thank you, mother. Thank you for understanding, you have indeed, been a wonderful parent."

"No need to thank me child, it was the least I could do. I only regret that I couldn't provide you with the sort of home and fortune that our family history warrants. But no matter, 'blame that on the ancestors', as my own mother would have said. There's no call for you to worry about me. I have friends in the village; I have my reading and my needlework to occupy my days. The truth is that, ever since you were old enough to take that job at the schoolhouse, my time has, for the most part, been my own. As I said, I knew this day would come eventually. Hoped that it would, in any case."

"I hope that it will be possible for me to secure a marriage proposal from him. After all, his intentions remain something of a mystery. But..... I must say that, if I am to marry, and marry for our family improvement, I am glad that he is a man that I find attractive. Although, I do feel rather terrible, plotting like this, to capture his attentions – it seems so cold a way to go about it."

"That is true enough, though he wouldn't be the first wealthy gentleman to fall for a pretty young governess."

Her mother smiled reassuringly.

"Don't worry you head about it being cold and calculating - marriages arranged in such a way are the standard thing amongst the *ton* – if it isn't you, he'll likely be forced to marry some chit he doesn't care for at all. Play your cards right my Cathy, and I shall be seeing somewhat less of you in the coming years. Do your family proud."

Catherine looked down into the stew, and tried to take a mouthful of the steaming stew. Try as she might, however, she could not seem to force the food down. She was too nervous, too distracted. Anticipation was building in her stomach.

She looked around at the small cottage she had known all her life. The thatch on the roof might be uneven, there might not be all that much room for two women, the bricks around the fireplace might have gone black over the years, but this was home - her home, which she had cherished, her refuge from the world.

It had always been her intention, someday, to move on from it, and yet now, looking at it and considering all that it meant to her, she was sad.

To be doing so, to take employment in an unfamiliar house, with a man she barely knew, yet whom she suspected she was falling in love with, made it doubly difficult.

There was a knock at the door. Catherine promptly abandoned her bowl of stew and went to open the door. It stuck a little, in its wooden frame, painted ultramarine blue, as worn as the rest of the cottage. Standing in front of her was a tall man with a thin, grave face and grey hair, dressed in livery.

He had lace at his cuffs, and a black velvet doublet, emblazoned with the coat of arms of the Stanningfield family.

This, she thought to herself, must be Featherstone.

"This is Hawthorn Cottage, in the village of Harteston?"

He peered inside to see Catherine's mother by the fireplace. He looked underwhelmed at the little cottage, but then, Catherine supposed, he was used to a stately home.

"Yes, indeed it is," she replied promptly.

"Then you, I presume, are Miss Catherine Thornberry?"

"I am."

"Very well. I am to escort you at once to Havisham Hall. My master informs me that he made an appointment with you earlier this afternoon."

"He did, yes."

With an acknowledging nod, Featherstone stepped to one side and gestured courteously for her to step through the door. She walked to the carriage with a sense of unreality, and was surprised again as, when she reached for the door, Featherstone spoke again.

"Please," he said in a serious tone of voice "-allow me."

Catherine was quite taken aback. She was unused to being served in this way. She had always had to run her own errands and carry her own luggage.

This was quite a new sensation, the feeling of being waited on. The simple act of opening a door had suddenly become something of significance.

She waited, bemused, as he let down the steps, opened the door, and ushered her in.

"Oh. Thank you very much, Mr…?"

"Featherstone," he said firmly, confirming that she was correct as to his identity. He paused, the door in his efficient, professional grasp. "I am the Steward of Havisham Hall, and I have served his Lordship for many years. I am not generally a coachman, these later years, but that's where I started, and I do enjoy the occasional excuse to drive."

His smile was infectious, and she found herself relaxing a little. She looked around the interior and was immediately struck by the plumpness of it, the finery.

"This is a magnificent coach. I have never before been in such a beautiful conveyance! I am not the wealthiest girl in the county, as I am sure you could have surmised."

His face lit up at her praise of the carriage, and he nodded cheerfully as he closed the door.

"Let us be on our way."

With that, he stepped away, and she felt the carriage rock as he climbed up and took the reins. Catherine lay back against the seat, and stared around her in amazement – here she had been wondering what wealth she would see in the Earl's house, and already the interior of the carriage outshone any house she had ever been inside!

There were silk cushions, plumped up and accommodating, and the softest upholstery she had ever had the pleasure to sit on.

The interior was decorated tastefully but richly, with gold renderings of the family crest on the two facing walls of the carriage.

Catherine could not help but gasp at the sheer luxury of it, and wondered how much it all must cost.

She placed her feet on a perfectly positioned foot rest, and looked out of the window to wave goodbye, not for the last time, but with a certain finality, to Hawthorn Cottage and the poor but contented life she might well be leaving for good, come tomorrow morning, if all went well with her interview with the Earl, and her meeting with his niece.

Her mother, convinced that Catherine would, indeed, leave her forever, come the morning, stood at the window wiping tears from the corners of her eyes, as the carriage pulled away.

Johnson sighed, his frustration with Charles' fidgeting evident in the sound, although he gave no other indication of anything out of the normal. Finally achieving a last tug of the cravat into place, he stepped back and eyed his master speculatively.

At home, Charles Rockingham was wont to be considerably less formal than most of the ton, and, even when preparing to interview a prospective governess, this seemed a little excessive a fuss about his appearance, compared to his usual behaviour. The Earl considered his appearance in the large mirror, which graced the wall of his dressing room, and nodded in satisfaction. He looked every bit the cool, in control Earl. A pity, he thought to himself, that he did not feel anything like that.

He was annoyed with himself – a man of thirty-two, with a history of very effectively seducing a range of delectable women, should not feel nervous about conducting an interview of a very ordinary village woman, however physically attractive he might find her.

Yet, ridiculous as it was, he found himself exactly that – nervous, unable to stand still, and worrying.

He was just worrying about this because the need for a governess was so desperate, that was it, surely that was all it was. What if she decided not to take the position? What if Theodora took one look and decided to hate her? He refused to consider that as an outcome. This must work. The mere thought of any of those terrible women, who had applied for the role by post, in response to his advertising, was enough to make him shudder.

He was, he assured himself, only concerned for Theodora – the fact that he wanted Miss Thornberry, that the image of her, soaked in river water, all her curves exposed to his gaze, haunted his thoughts, had nothing to do with the nervousness.

Nothing at all.

Charles strode down the hallway to Theodora's room and tapped firmly on the door, entering when the maid pulled the door open. At 14 Theodora was beginning to see herself as rather grown up, and to demand that she be treated that way – when of course, she remembered.... She was still child enough to be easily distracted by kittens, and toys at times.

She was what some might call wilful, a characteristic which Charles chose to see more as an indicator of her strong character - character that reminded him all too much of himself at the same age.

Smiling at him, in a way that was almost able to be interpreted as impertinent, but not quite, she dipped an elegant curtsey to him.

"Good afternoon, sir."

Her voice was clear, and reminded him of her mother's – a voice made for singing, for bringing those hearing it to awe of its beauty.

He shook the moment of sadness away – that was the past.

"Good afternoon, Theodora, I am glad to see that you are ready, and suitably presented. Please come downstairs and wait in the blue parlour. I will speak to Miss Thornberry in the drawing room first, and then, if I feel that she will suit, I will call for you to come and meet her." Seeing a frown start to take shape on Theodora's face, he continued speaking, hoping to prevent its settling into place. "I pray you, do not make any assumptions about her until you meet her – being judgemental about a person that you have not met is very impolite, and most unladylike. I think that you will be pleasantly surprised."

That last comment was enough to make Theodora pause – surely any woman working as a governess would be stern and harsh, with no sense of humour and nothing to like about her? Still, she had come to know that, even though the Earl could be impetuous, even occasionally prone to temper, he was, at heart, a very honest man.

She had good reason to know that he hated subterfuge, and would be open and fair if he possibly could.

Nodding her acquiescence, Theodora let the frown dissipate, and followed him out of the door, and down the elegant, sweeping stairs.

With Theodora settled in the blue parlour, accompanied by her maid, and supplied with tea and scones to keep her occupied, Charles took himself to the drawing room to wait. Waiting proved trying. He could not settle, and his nervous energy drove him to pace, rather like a horse stabled too long, that needed to gallop out its tensions.

He alternately stared out the windows across the terrace to the gardens, and paced across the room, listening for any sound of the carriage returning. With difficulty, he resisted the urge to run his hand through his hair, or to tug at his cravat – ruining Johnson's artistry would not help him make a good, and convincing impression on Miss Thornberry.

And yes, he realised, he wanted her good opinion. That a peer of the realm should care for the opinion of a schoolmistress was not at all normal, but he did. He assured himself, yet again, that it was just because he needed to solve the governess problem. It was, however, getting harder to believe his own assurances.

He eyed the brandy decanter, where it sat on the sideboard, and then turned away – maybe later – for now, he needed to be clearheaded. Another five circuits of the room, and he feared that he was wearing a path in the carpet (which was Aubusson, and a family treasure), when, finally, he heard the crunch of gravel beneath the carriage wheels, as it drew up at the front of the house.

He strode out, calling the key staff to attend, and went to the doors.

# Chapter Eight

Catherine watched the familiar countryside from inside the carriage, trying with all her might not to break or dirty anything. That would have been a most inauspicious start to her new employment, assuming that this interview resulted in her being employed, which was, perhaps, presumptuous of her. She was determined to make a good impression, and to not give off the sense that she was unused to this sort of high life, and to wealth. She supposed that was silly as he knew of her circumstances, yet she felt the need to not appear common and poor.

She might have been born and raised in a humble cottage without much wealth behind her, but she was from a great family going way back, and this sort of thing ought not to overwhelm her too much.

Nevertheless, the stew pot by the fireside and the often grubby-faced children in the crumbling village schoolhouse all suddenly seemed a very long way away. The little stew that she had managed to eat sat in a leaden lump in her stomach, and nervousness made her feel mildly ill. But along with that, a growing excitement infected her, a fluttering in her stomach, pushing the lump of stew aside, was the result of just the thought of seeing him again.

Her mother might want her to capture the Earl's affections for the family honour, but she found that she was just as interested in capturing his affections for herself. Never before had a man made her feel like this, and the warmth that flooded her body at the memory of his arms around her on the horse, of his lips against hers in that kiss, was a disturbingly pleasant sensation.

She looked in greater detail at her immediate surroundings. This was the first real opportunity she had had to get a look at the Earl of Stanningfield's crest, and she was most impressed by it. A great shield in the shape of a kite was at the centre of it, with an oak tree, tall and proud in the middle, three little gold balls she knew to call 'besants' assembled over it. Above these was a strip, and in that field five three-pointed stars. Around the edges of the shield was an intricate design formed by thorns and laurel leaves, curving symmetrically around the edges.

These were held in place by two mythical beasts, griffins she thought, with the wings and heads of eagles but the bodies of lions. Magnificent creatures, proud and mighty, much like Charles Rockingham himself. At the bottom in a curling scroll read the family motto: *Fortitudine et Honorem.*

She knew enough Latin, from her study of what books she could get, to know what that meant: 'strength and honour'.

A simple motto for an ancient family. Looking at the great coat-of-arms she dared herself to think that a de Quincey panther might complement the design nicely. Maybe at some point in the near future, she thought to herself.

Outside, the landscape rolled by at a pleasing pace. She was not used to travelling at this speed, having walked everywhere for the bulk of her twenty-four years, but she could still make out familiar sights. The late afternoon light shone on fields of golden wheat, ripening in the May sun. In a few months' time, all of the fields around would be consumed by all the busy activity of the harvest - with gangs of boys running behind the haywains, sweating out their day's labour. There were trees as well, many oaks and elms, tall, green and mighty. They broke up the monotony of all the rolling fields and gentle hills, looming over the crops and the haystacks. The trees were resplendent in their summery finery, so many shades of green; emerald, shamrock, Kelly, viridian and Lincoln. England, she thought, was not such a bad country on a fine day such as today. What a balmy and beautiful early summer evening to be going up to Havisham Hall to meet her new life.

She heard the wheels of the carriage crunching on gravel, and presumed that they must have reached their destination. They came to a halt, and Featherstone opened the carriage door, lowered the steps and helped her down.

She was indeed correct, they had arrived at the most splendid house that she had ever had the privilege of seeing. Two ornately carved balustrades converged on a single, elegant rise of steps leading upwards, towards the front door. Assembled around it was at least part of the household staff, what appeared to be the Butler, the Housekeeper, and a number of footmen, standing to an obedient attention waiting for her.

The idea of it shocked her – surely she did not merit such a welcome. The house was at least five stories high, and she tried to count the number of windows running across each floor, each pair seemingly a single room. She quickly lost count, and started to feel rather giddy at the vastness of the place. The entire front façade was beautifully plastered in a creamy white and yellow and above the main entranceway a stern plaque, held aloft by two marble-carved cherubs, proclaimed once again the family motto, *Fortitudine et Honorem*.

The grounds were all as wonderfully well-kept as the house itself, manicured lawns in two rich shades of green. The trees tastefully dispersed across the meticulously kept grounds appeared to extend for many acres around. She could see an enormous fountain in the near distance by the entrance to a yew-tree maze, and over on the other side in the distance a fine little pagoda by a duck pond. Such splendour!

What wealth this man and his family must possess! What a wonderful home! Standing in front of all of it, offering a hand and a charming smile, as confident as ever in his stance and posture, was the lord of the manor, Charles Rockingham, third Earl of Stanningfield, stepping out from between his servants to welcome her, Miss Catherine Thornberry!

"So good of you to come," he said finally, stooping to kiss her hand. "I hope that my humble abode is to your satisfaction."

"Sir, it is the most wonderful house I have ever had the privilege of being invited to!"

For a moment Catherine abandoned all composure. She was taken aback, awestruck by Havisham Hall and all the majesty it seemed to promise. Any pretence of sophistication, that such things seemed normal to her, was stripped away.

"It is most kind of you to say so," the Earl was as cool and composed as ever. "I've recently had the façade re-plastered; the old place was starting to look a little shabby. I'm having the grounds remodelled as well; they are currently set down to my grandfather's tastes, which I regret to confess I do not myself share."

"I cannot even begin to imagine how one could go about improving such a house!" Catherine gasped. "To me, it already seems more perfect than I had ever imagined any home could be!"

"You flatter me. However, when you have passed the great bulk of your life in a place such as I have here, I suppose it starts to seem a little dull to you." He turned her to the side, and motioned his staff forward. "Miss Thornberry, this is Wilton, my Butler, and Mrs Cartwright, my Housekeeper." She acknowledged the bow and curtsey that they gave her, feeling rather overwhelmed by it all, and turned back towards the Earl. "Now let us not tarry, come, we have business to conduct."

Without a moment's hesitation he placed his gloved hand on the small of her back and urged her up the steps, into the interior of Havisham Hall.

On the inside the house was, of course, just as splendid. It was exactly as Catherine had always imagined a stately home such as this to be, only more so. To actually be here, and seeing it in person, taking in all of its antique delights, she was quite overwhelmed. A marble staircase led up to the top floors, with rich blue carpet draped over its central axis, inviting one upwards. The floor was remarkable, an austere black and white, polished to a sheen she had not even imagined to be possible.

The decoration was remarkably tasteful, the Earl had evidently dispensed with the centuries of aristocratic clutter, which she had always presumed would decorate a house like this, in favour of simplicity and grace.

There was a great clock standing at the centre of the landing above the staircase, gilt-edged and superbly rendered, solemnly ticking away. Two enormous mirrors sat either side of the entranceway, and Catherine turned, to see her entire body perfectly reflected back, for the very first time in her life.

She was amazed, and then instantly felt conscious of the simplicity of her own dress. Despite wearing the very best that she owned, a dark green frock that she had always considered to be elegant, next to all of this finery, and to the Earl's superbly tailored clothing, she felt a little shabby and ashamed. She turned away from the mirror and saw, by the side of the stairs, a massive portrait of the Earl, Charles Rockingham, striking a powerful pose with his hand on his hip and a hunting dog at his side, grinning in that casual, mischievous way of his.

"There I am of course," he said proudly. "We used to have a portrait of my ancestor, the first Earl of Stanningfield, in this position, but I must confess I couldn't bear to look at the old boy every day. Do you think the artist has captured my likeness?"

"Oh, very much so, my Lord. Why it is as if you yourself were sitting in the picture frame, regaling us with your smile."

"I am pleased to hear you say so. Regrettably I had to dispose of the services of the first artist I employed. He was technically gifted, but he wanted me to pose in the nude, like one of those Roman or Greek fellows. Most unorthodox, all I required was a straightforward portrait, fit for the present age, such as this one here."

Catherine did everything she could not to giggle nervously at the thought of the Earl posing naked.

She pictured it vividly, the mighty thighs, the strapping chest, the bare and impressive manhood.

(Well, what she thought such a thing would look like – she did not exactly have anything to go by! Occasional glimpses of the village boys swimming in the stream when they though no-one was looking did not provide much of a reference).

It required all of her powers of concentration not to blush red all over with excited embarrassment. The flutter at the base of her stomach, and the tightening of her breasts as she imagined it were most distracting.

"Let us go into the drawing room," the Earl declared. "We can discuss the position, and the necessary arrangements in comfort there."

He led her into the next room, and once again it was all Catherine could do to stop herself from gasping in awe. The drawing room was immense, and so airy and sophisticated in its design. The high-ceiling and great windows on one side gave one the impression, almost, of being outdoors, whilst yet remaining in the warmth and comfort of the house. Everything was fresh, light, and open, and she could feel herself smiling at the wonder of it. A wooden parquet floor stretched across the entire room, once again polished to shimmer like water. To one side was a long elegantly upholstered couch, an equally elegant small table set before it, and a pretty silver dish atop a lace covering upon it. In the centre of the room was a magnificent Aubusson carpet, well placed to be lit by the spectacular crystal chandelier that hung above.

At the other side of the room were several chairs and couches, plusher and more inviting than any she had ever sat on, assembled around smaller tables, and set to allow the warmth of the fireplace to reach them in winter. The entire room was designed so that the chairs and couches afforded a view through the huge windows, to the gardens beyond.

The Earl ushered her to a chair, close to the windows on that side, and then sank onto the chair beside her, once she was settled.

"Can I offer you something to drink? It may be a little late for tea, but I have plenty to offer you. Some Madeira, or a lighter wine? I am told that Featherstone has recently acquired a superb Champagne that I could have brought up from the cellar – I believe it is the latest rage for the ladies of the *ton* - if you would like a glass of wine?"

"Oh, I do not think it would be proper of me to indulge in strong beverages at such an important meeting. Tea will suffice for me."

"Are you quite sure? You are more than welcome to make yourself comfortable; if we come to an agreement, and you feel that you can care for Theodora, then you are to be living here permanently as my niece's new governess, after all."

"I appreciate your generosity my Lord, but I fear it would be best for me to stick to tea."

"Very well."

He reached out and pulled the rope which hung to the side of the window, to summon one of the servants. A middle-aged woman with a thick-set brow appeared in a maid's uniform at the entrance to the drawing room.

"Yes, my Lord?"

She was working hard to conceal her Suffolk accent.

"Polly, would you be so kind as to bring some tea for our guest?"

"Of course sir, at once."

She disappeared promptly to fetch the tea. The Earl rose to his feet and went over immediately to the drinks cabinet to the side of the room. As he spoke, he poured himself a glass of a brown liquid, which Catherine took to be brandy, from a crystal decanter.

"You will forgive me if I indulge in a little brandy, Miss Thornberry?"

"Of course."

At that moment, Polly returned with the tea, and placed it on the table beside her, eyes bright with curiosity. The Earl waited until Polly had left the room before he continued.

"Good. Now I believe that I laid out the essentials of the position, which I am offering you, in our rather... extraordinary meeting at the schoolhouse in Harteston."

"Yes sir, indeed you did."

"It is pleasing to see that you were paying attention then. In brief, you would be required to attend, six days a week, to educating my young niece, Theodora. As I have previously informed you, she is a most pleasant girl who is simply in need of the hand of a capable governess. I infer from your professional employment that you would be more than qualified to undertake such a task. I will, of course, offer you a salary more than adequate – significantly more than the parish has been able to pay you. I will also offer to supply your mother with a more than adequate quantity of food, delivered each week, from Havisham Hall's supplies. I would not wish you to be concerned for her, without you there to care for her."

He turned, glass in hand, and walked back across the room, to stand directly in front of her.

"All that I really require from you Miss Thornberry…" Now he was looking directly at her, standing so close to her. His eyes were the same colour as the brandy in his glass. She felt her pulse quicken at the proximity, a stirring beneath her petticoats, a flutter in her stomach, "… is a firm commitment, once you have met Theodora. The position would require you to leave your current post as schoolmistress, and to come and live permanently at Havisham Hall." A jolt of pleasure ran through her. So, he was serious! She could move into this wonderful house and begin a new life! But was he serious about her? Would yesterday's kiss ever be repeated? "Are you in agreement Miss Thornberry? Is this position one that you can see yourself taking?"

Catherine paused, her heart beating fast, and thought – she could not really refuse – it would mean her mother's care assured, and so much more money for herself – enough to truly improve both their lives. And, truth to tell, she did not want to refuse, she wanted to be near this man, more than was proper, more than she should, but she wanted it nonetheless.

"Yes, my Lord, I believe that I could be happy in such a position."

"Most Excellent!"

He spun away a moment, and deposited his glass on the table. Again, he tugged on the bell pull, as Catherine carefully poured herself tea into the beautiful, delicate china cup that she had been given, and sipped to ease her nerves.

Polly reappeared, and was asked to bring Miss Theodora to the room. Moments later, the door opened to admit a young girl, a girl on the verge of womanhood. She was tall, and showing signs of great beauty to come. Her figure was still childishly slim, but the hints of curves were beginning to show.

Her hair was dark, but not as dark as the Earl's, full of gold and reddish highlights as the light touched it, where it was drawn back in a simple knot.

"Come in, Theodora. Miss Thornberry, may I present Miss Theodora Rockingham, my niece. Theodora, this is Miss Catherine Thornberry. It is my intention that Miss Thornberry become your governess. I have asked you to come here so that you might meet each other, before we finalise that arrangement. I realise that most guardians would simply employ someone, without consulting you in any way, but I choose to be unconventional – I would prefer that you actually get on with your governess."

Theodora dipped into a suitably polite curtsey, then stood and raised her eyes to Catherine's face. They were startling eyes, of an intense green, with flecks of blue, unlike anything that Catherine had ever seen. The effect was breath-taking, in the pale, beautiful face. Catherine smiled, captivated. This was no milksop aristocratic miss – there was intelligence, curiosity, and character in that face.

"Good afternoon Miss Theodora, I am most pleased to meet you."

Catherine's voice was as warm as her smile. Perhaps, she thought, this role could be more pleasant than she had ever imagined – for surely this was a girl with a thirst for life, who would learn, and want to learn, although, perhaps, not always the things that young ladies were expected to learn! Theodora's eyes widened at Catherine's friendly tone, and her words came without apparent thought.

"You are not at all what I expected, Miss Thornberry!" The Earl tapped his foot, looking at Theodora with some mild annoyance. "Oh, I am sorry Miss Thornberry. I do sometimes speak before I think! I was just so surprised."

Theodora blushed a little, and her eyes flicked to the Earl for a moment. Catherine's eyes followed, and discovered a fleeting expression of amusement cross his face, before it went back to calm and impassive.

"I…. well, I rather expected a governess to be older, and somewhat more… stern."

She sounded so confused by the fact that Catherine was not like that, that Catherine found herself laughing – a clear joyful sound that startled both Theodora and Charles, then brought a smile to their faces.

"Thank you, Theodora, thank you! I have no wish to be old and stern. Thank you for being honest and telling me your thoughts – although, perhaps, for polite society, you may need to curb that tendency a little – the *ton* are not often forgiving." Charles looked on, making no comment on this interaction, but Catherine was sure that she saw him relax, saw the tension drop out of his shoulders – perhaps he really had been worried what she and Theodora would think of each other. This was not, in her opinion, the behaviour of a hardened rake. "So, Miss Theodora, do you think that you could stand to have me as your governess? That we could go along together well?

Theodora stood thinking, hesitating, then suddenly flung her arms around Catherine, in the sort of hug that one would expect from a small lost child. Startled, Catherine froze a moment, then gently eased her arms around Theodora. In a small, slightly shaky voice Theodora spoke into Catherine's shoulder.

"Oh yes, please, Miss Catherine, I have been so lonely since Gran died. I so want to have someone to talk to, to help me. I promise to even really try to learn – yes, even the things I hate learning – please do say yes, Miss Catherine."

Smiling at Charles, over the top of Theodora's tousled head, Catherine spoke.

"Yes Theodora, yes my Lord, I will take the position. I think that Theodora and I will rub along famously together. Let us conclude the formal arrangements, so that I may return here to take up the role as soon as possible."

Theodora relaxed against her at the words, and, as Catherine gently stroked her hair, lifted her head, those amazing eyes positively glowing.

"Thank you, Miss Catherine, thank you."

She stood back, a little embarrassed now at her actions, but smiling still.

"Thank you Theodora." The Earl's voice was warm, his expression relieved. "Now please go and finish your tea, whilst Miss Thornberry and I sort out the arrangements."

Theodora curtseyed again, then positively bounced out of the room. It was the happiest that Charles had seen her look since Mrs Walsh's death. Charles went to Catherine, and took her hands.

She felt a little frisson run through her at his touch, and looked into his face with wonder. When he spoke, his voice was deep, and she felt some great emotion in him, just below the surface.

"I did not expect that, but I am more than happy that it happened that way. This lifts a great weight from my mind, for I genuinely care a great deal about Theodora. Most unfashionable for a guardian, I know, but there it is. Come, let us be seated and complete our agreement."

He turned, and led her to the couch, still holding her hand.

Catherine was intensely aware of him, of the heat of his hand on hers, of the scent of him, a heady mixture of brandy and something herbal, like sage – he must be wearing a cologne of some sort – all underlaid by the tantalising musk of the male body.

She shivered a little, remembering that kiss again, wanting, if she was honest with herself, for him to kiss her again.

She sat on the couch, and he stepped to the sideboard, picking up a sheet of paper that lay there, then came to sit beside her.

"I am, as I said, very happy that you have chosen to accept the position. I had hoped that you would do so, and that Theodora would be at least accepting. So, this has worked out considerably better than I had hoped. I am sure that you will be happy here. I will do everything in my power to make it so." He watched her as he spoke, those brandy-coloured eyes sparkling. "I have taken the liberty of drafting a letter informing the parish that you have accepted alternative employment. All that it requires is your signature..." He leaned in closer to her, smiling in that way that made her feel quite breathless, and placed the letter in her hands. She could feel his breath falling on her, see the lines where he had shaved his shapely jaw – she felt an irrational desire to run her finger along that line. "...and I will interpret that as a commitment, to me, and to the position as Theodora's governess. Here is an employment agreement between us, which I have already signed, in the hopeful expectation that you would be accepting the role."

He turned away, and produced the second paper from his pocket, and placed it in her hands.

Catherine quickly scanned the letter to the parish:

*Dear Sirs,*

*I regret to inform you that I leave the position of schoolmistress at Harteston Parish School vacant, with immediate effect. I have been offered alternative employment elsewhere, as a governess, and have decided to take up this new position. I have every confidence that you will find a suitable replacement in a very short time. Please convey my condolences to the children; I am sorry that I could not see their schooling to its conclusion.*

*Yours faithfully,*

*Catherine Thornberry*

She looked up.

The letter was blunter than she might have made it, but it communicated the point. Catherine looked out of the window at the splendid grounds, around the magnificent drawing room, and into the handsome face of the Earl.

Without another moment's hesitation, she took up the pen that was sitting on the small table, and inscribed her signature onto the bottom of the letter.

Turning to the other papers, the agreement for her employment, she gasped, raising shocked eyes to his, when she read the promised amount of her wages. It was much more than she had ever expected – more than anything else, it made the vast gap between their stations obvious to her.

To him, this amount was unimportant – easily paid, as just a minor expense. To her, it was a life transforming amount.

It was also much more than she believed governesses were usually paid.

Doubts assailed her – was he simply generous? Or did this payment presage an expectation of what he might want from her, beyond the tasks of a governess? Shaking the doubts aside, she signed – it was too late for doubt, and she had discovered today, with Theodora's arms around her, that she wanted to be here, no matter what. And, if her mother's wishes came true, and she should manage to engage the Earl's affections, deeply enough for marriage, then she would not be at all unhappy about that either.

She handed him the papers. He smiled, and offered her further tea, which she declined, suddenly in a hurry to get back to Hawthorn Cottage, to pack up the last of her small collection of belongings, to prepare for tomorrow.

The Earl stood, and bowed to her, graceful and elegant, then took her hand and assisted her to rise. He pulled her towards him, a little more than necessary, and steadied her with a hand on her waist. She stilled, so close to him, her eyes caught by his, his rich masculine scent filling her nostrils, her heart beating hard. She dragged her eyes away from his, only to have them fix on his lips – those full, firm lips that she had felt on hers, but a few days ago. Her breathing became ragged, and her eyes fluttered half closed. She wanted him to kiss her again. Now.

He was so close, his breath brushed her lips, as she unconsciously licked her tongue across them. Somehow, the distance between them had disappeared, she felt the hardness of his chest against the softness of hers, and the heat of his body warming hers. His lips came down on hers softly, his tongue tracing the contours of her mouth, until she moaned a little sound of pleasure. As her lips parted, so his tongue slipped between them, exploring and caressing the warm cavern of her mouth.

He made a small sound, almost a sound of desperation, and crushed her hard against him, the kiss becoming deeper, demanding. The world melted away, there was nothing but him, his body against hers. Then, suddenly, he pulled away.

"I apologise Miss Thornberry, I should not have... It is inappropriate for me to impose myself on you. You should go – you need to get back to your mother, and arrange your things. I will have the carriage brought around."

His look was regretful, but full of desire, and she thought about it all the way home.

The memory of the kiss haunted Charles throughout the evening, and kept him awake at night. If he had wanted her before, he wanted her doubly so now.

Yet he should not.

She was an innocent, she was now his employee, damn it, and Theodora needed her – more than he had realised.

His mind might rationalise it, but his body disagreed – he lay in bed, unable to stop thinking about her, his cock achingly hard, even after he had given himself some relief earlier. This may be the best thing for Theodora, but if he continued this way, it might make him quite mad.

He was not used to not being able to have a woman that he wanted.

To add to it all, he reminded himself, he was betrothed.

The fact that, for the last three days, that reality had completely escaped his mind, was a rather damning reflection on how he felt about Lady Blanchette. He did not wish to dishonour Catherine, yet he wanted her. Again, he realised, with a sense of shame, it reflected poorly on him that he had so easily taken Blanchette's virtue, yet he did not want to dishonour Catherine.

He chose to see that as an indication that he was growing more responsible, less of a rake. For to see it as anything else was unthinkable, was something fraught with so much complication that it could not be considered. None of which made any difference to the fact that he wanted Catherine more than he had ever wanted any woman since Monique. Mentally, he shied away from the possible implications of that thought, and brought himself back to thinking of the most boring things that he could, in the hope of finding sleep.

Eventually, exhaustion took him, and he slept, all too short a time before Johnson came to wake him, and prepare him for the day. Once he was assured that Mrs Cartwright had prepared a suitable room for Catherine, not too far from Theodora's, in the servants' section of the same floor of the house, and that everything was in readiness for her arrival, he asked Featherstone to arrange the carriage to collect her.

Featherstone again volunteered to drive, and Charles smiled, willing to let him do something below his standing in the household, simply because it pleased his loyal retainer to do so.

~~~~~
~~~~~

Catherine stood near the fire, watching her mother, who sat, determinedly keeping herself occupied with sewing, staving off her tears by force of will. Mother had been happy to hear that Theodora was a child who needed love and care, who wanted to cooperate – for she could not imagine anything worse than trying to teach a child who had no interest in every doing anything that you wanted.

But still, the thought that she would only see Catherine occasionally was hard to deal with right now. Catherine felt the same – they had cried in each other's arms the previous night – both sad and happy tears. For now there was a chance that Catherine might engage the Earl's affections, and, even if that did not happen, between the money that he would pay Catherine, and the food stuffs that he had promised would be delivered to the Cottage, this would be the first year since Catherine was born that Mother could be certain they would not starve, even if she did no paid sewing for anyone else.

It was an odd thought to have even that much security, after so many years of just scraping through.

Catherine's small collection of possessions were gathered near the door, waiting for the carriage to come and collect her. It was, when all brought together, a pitifully small amount of things. Compared to what was in the huge house that she was going to, this might as well be nothing – but it was all she had. Her few dresses and other clothing, her sewing basket, and her small collection of precious books.

She turned as she heard steps on the path, and opened the door before Featherstone reached it.

"Good morning Miss Thornberry." Featherstone smiled, and looked around. Spotting her luggage, he turned back to her, an expression of surprise on his face. "Is this all, Miss?"

Embarrassed, she looked down, twisting her hands in her skirt, then took a deep breath and answered.

"Yes Featherstone, this is all. We have never been wealthy enough for more."

His expression shifted to sadness, and his voice was kind when he spoke.

"You've done very well with what you have, and I know that the parish children are the better for your teaching. As will Miss Theodora be. We are all so glad that she took to you – she can be a handful, but she has a good heart. She's been too sad since old Mrs Walsh went."

She nodded, brought to the edge of tears again by the unexpected kindness. He took up her meagre possessions, and she turned to hug her mother yet again, promising to come and visit very soon, then turned and walked to the carriage, before the tears took hold again.

Her mother stood in the doorway, watching, until the carriage was out of sight. She walked back in, closing the door softly and stood a moment, looking at the de Quincey family tree. Then, in a whisper barely above silent, she spoke, before turning back to her sewing.

"Oh mama, grandmamma, and my dear grand aunt, maybe there is hope yet, maybe Catherine can restore what we lost, what I so foolishly threw away."

# Chapter Ten

"But Miss Thornberry," squealed Theodora "I don't understand, why should I have to learn another silly language like French? I can talk in English perfectly nicely, my Gran said so herself."

Catherine sighed. It had been a week now. A week in which she had barely seen the Earl, after he had greeted her on her arrival, and provided her with a maid and a footman to assist her with getting settled in.

It almost felt as if he was avoiding her, and she worried that he regretted that kiss in the drawing room so much that he could not bear to see her.

It was a depressing thought.

She had been given two small rooms in the servants' section of this floor, quite close should Theodora need her, but enough to give her some privacy.

Even though the rooms were small for this house, they were still bigger than the whole of Hawthorn Cottage. With just her tiny collection of possessions in them, they felt oddly empty. They had no personality yet, and she had nothing more to put there, to make them feel homely.

Ah well, that could come with time. For now, she needed to deal with Theodora's frustrated stubbornness.

On days like this, it seemed that her new post might not be quite as easy as she had hoped. Theodora was, as the Earl had said, and as she had seen when she met her, a pleasant enough girl, but she was stubborn, and obstinate at times, and had no desire to learn anything that did not interest her.

"There are ample reasons, my dear," she replied wearily. "All the pretty young ladies in society know a little French, so that they may converse with gentlemen. You won't ever find yourself a suitable husband if you can't express yourself in the French tongue."

"I don't believe you!" the child fairly shouted back. "Why on earth should that be the case! We're English after all, therefore we speak English. Why should we waste our time learning all these other ways of speaking?"

Catherine looked around the nursery. Her surroundings did not offer much inspiration for responding to the girl's questions, but they were pleasant enough.

Theodora was passing her girlhood in far greater comfort and splendour than she herself could ever have imagined.

Although, thinking about it, she realised that she had heard that Theodora had only come here, to the Earl's wardship, about three years ago. That, before that, she had lived somewhere distant, in lesser circumstances.

Idly, she wondered where. Catherine wished that, when she had been a child, she had had such wonderful toys. Theodora's toys were most splendid: beautiful china dolls in real silk dresses, a superbly carved rocking horse, and the most ornate doll's house with every imaginable detail and accessory. The room was perfectly laid out for a young girl, with a light shade of pink on the walls and big bright windows offering views of the countryside all around. Still, what had been appropriate for a girl of ten or eleven, was daily becoming less appropriate for a girl of fourteen, growing fast towards womanhood.

Despite, or perhaps because of, all this, Theodora was no scholar.

She looked for any opportunity to get out of her studies. She was bright, and quite capable, but most study did not interest her – she would rather run in the gardens, play with puppies in the stables or sneak into the kitchens and get her fingers into whatever cook was making. It made life an interesting challenge for Catherine.

"Imagine for a moment..." Catherine replied at last "...that in the near future you are given the opportunity to go on a trip, the Grand Tour, to France, perhaps with an Aunt or other older relative. On your travels you will surely encounter some interesting French persons of distinction and quality; perhaps some handsome young gentlemen you wish to converse with."

Theodora stared at her, the stubborn expression as yet unchanged.

"Now, tell me Miss Theodora, how frustrating would it be to find that you could not speak to them, or understand a single word that they said? Would that not be terribly annoying? Would you not wish that you had listened to Miss Thornberry and practised your French, back in your nursery, were such a situation to arise?"

"No. I think not."

"Pray tell, why?"

"Because I cannot imagine any French person has anything of interest to say to me. I am English, and I will have English friends, who are perfectly capable of speaking to me in English. That is all that there is to say."

"But there are also many interesting books that you will not be capable of reading if you do not learn French, books that your beloved English friends may have read, and which they may wish to discuss, and which you will be unable to comment upon."

"If that is to be the case then so be it. I doubt that there are any interesting books in French anyway, and anyone who would want to read them would be nothing but a dullard."

Catherine was on the point of furnishing a response to this when suddenly her thoughts were interrupted by a voice from the door:

"Theodora, stop aggravating your new governess so, it isn't polite."

It was the Earl, dressed far more casually than was proper, in a flattering shirt, which was unlaced enough to reveal a triangle of skin at his throat, and with only a waistcoat over it, leaning against the door frame and smiling at both of them. Catherine was briefly worried that her heart was going to leap out of its place in her chest; it picked up its rate of beating so suddenly.

She suppressed a gasp of delight and turned to face him.

"My Lord! I thought you'd gone out?"

"I thought I'd give old Thaddeus a rest today. Been riding him pretty hard of late, I don't want to risk injuring the horse."

"That is most kind of you."

"Indeed, I can be generous, on occasion. I hope that Theodora hasn't been giving you too much trouble?"

"No indeed, she has been most obedient - although we were just in the midst of a dispute about the various merits of studying the French language."

"*Quand j'etais petit, j'ai appris beaucoup de la langue Francaise, et elle m'a servit tres bien*. There. What did I just say to you Theodora?"

The girl looked sheepishly down at her feet, embarrassed by her ignorance.

"I don't know," she mumbled in response, blushing.

"There. Now if you don't want to grow up feeling like that all the time you'd best get your nose in some books pretty sharpish. Have we a French-English dictionary in the nursery?"

"Indeed, we do," said Catherine. "I was just about to set Theodora some exercises from it."

"Then we have all of the pedagogical resources we require. In that case, you won't feel any guilt if you leave Theodora in the nursery for the present time and come and take a walk with me around the grounds. We wouldn't want you to waste away in here all your days, would we?"

With that Catherine felt her heart lurch upwards once more, and a fluttering in her belly which she could not contain.

So that was why he was here!

What a charming interjection, she was quite overcome! Yet, why now, after she had barely seen him for days? He did not seem in any way sensible, but a part of her most definitely did not care for sense. She felt flushed, nervous, and excited, and quivery in ways that she had never felt before.

"Yes sir," she said, quite calmly. "I think that would be quite agreeable, provided you do not think your niece's schooling assumes a higher priority?"

"Indeed not, she needs to learn some self-discipline. Get down to your studies Theodora, or your place in high society might be forfeit. And that would be a great pity, given what your family went through, to ensure you the opportunity that you have."

Theodora nodded seriously in response. It was obvious to Catherine that there was something more complex behind the words, some shared knowledge between the Earl and Theodora, something that Theodora cared enough about, to change her behaviour for. At least for now.

The Earl held out his arm firmly to Catherine, and she took it without a second's pause.

"Now you've no excuse. You simply must come and take a walk with me in the grounds. It's disgraceful that you have been here over a week, and I have not yet shown you the beautiful gardens – I have been remiss." And with that they were off.

# Chapter Eleven

Up close the grounds were even lovelier than she had imagined they could be. Catherine had never seen grass so well-kept, or flower beds so carefully planted and maintained. They walked arm in arm through a charming little rose garden. On either side of them, banks of red, white, and gold flowers grew high and haughty, and let off a rich scent.

"I suppose much of this must be quite new to you," he said, pausing for a moment to sniff the head of an especially tall flower. It was vast and bright red, and the smell was evidently pleasing to him. "Theodora loves this garden, but she will only sit here by herself, and she won't tell me why."

He sounded frustrated by this, but did not say anything further about it.

"It certainly is new to me," she confessed readily. "We have a little garden back at our cottage in Harteston where mother has always liked to cultivate herbs for cooking, and a few pretty flowers, but nothing of this sort."

"That sounds charming, in its own way. I am unused to small houses or modest gardens. I suppose I take all of this…" he waved around him to indicate the grounds of Havisham Hall "…for granted. Ever since I was small I have been surrounded by splendour, and by a large and dedicated staff. Do you know that it takes twenty men, employed full-time, all year round, to keep all of this horticulture in order? I suppose it is pleasant enough, but a great deal of effort and expense goes into maintaining all of this pleasantness."

"Pleasant? The word does not do it justice. It is positively beautiful, the whole thing."

"You are generous in your description. I have seen greater gardens in my time; the grounds of the Palace of Versailles for instance, or at Leeds Castle, down in Kent. But my own little parcel of England is pretty enough in its own right, of course. Have you travelled at all, Miss Thornberry?"

"I'm afraid not."

"No, I suppose your instructional duties at the school would not have permitted it. It is good to see a little of the world if one has the chance. I have been fortunate enough to voyage far and wide in my time, and it is true what they say, it does broaden the mind. But then I suppose you have your reading for that?"

"Yes, I do. Reading can open up new experiences and possibilities as well."

"I imagine that it can, though I have rarely taken great pleasure in it myself. I did, however, look into this Fielding fellow whom you recommended to me. I have ordered a copy of his *Tom Jones* from a publisher in London, and I am looking forward to commencing reading it."

Catherine was quite taken aback! To think that she, a plain and simple girl as she was, had already had some effect on the mind and habits of this great and noble gentleman! How was it even possible? She thought now of other changes that she might effect in his character, if, as it seemed, she had some strange power of influence over him.

Perhaps she could turn him away from his reputed rough and roguish ways towards the affairs of the mind, the heart, and the soul. It would be both a satisfying and a remarkable effort.

They had come to rest on a simple but sturdy bench in the shade of a great oak tree. It was a rather impressive tree, possibly the largest that Catherine had ever seen. It towered above them, and its bark was tight, hard and sinewy. She brushed her back against it and could feel the roughness of it, tough and turgid, but pleasing, nonetheless. It was one of many new sensations that she seemed to be experiencing now, all at once.

"Tell me..." said the Earl in his languid manner. "...this innkeeper's boy, who you have mentioned to me as your sweetheart, how advanced is the affair between the two of you?"

"I must confess sir, most of that was a fabrication. I am familiar with the boy in question, and have been since I was a girl. He is, as you say, a most attractive young man, but it would be dishonest of me to claim that there was anything of significance between us."

"I see," he said with a chuckle. "So you lied to me because you knew it would provoke my interest?"

"Oh no sir, not a lie…"

"There is no need to protest, Catherine," he said, calling her by her first name for the very first time. He was leaning very close to her, looking her straight in the eye. Catherine felt her heart pounding away inside her breast, so close to his that she wondered whether he could hear it or not. Immediately her mind went back to that last kiss in the drawing room, to the feel of his body against hers. Desire trickled through her, making her feel weak and shaky. Her hands were damp, and she shivered slightly in anticipation, and the hope that he would kiss her again. She wanted to feel that way again, to taste and feel him, no matter how wanton that might make her. "I know young ladies and their fey and fickle ways. I can forgive you. In fact, I rather admire you for it."

And with that, he broke his charming grin and leaned forward, like an inevitable force, until his lips met hers. The kiss started gently, but she could feel the full vigour of his passion in it. She melted against him, wanting this, even whilst she knew that she should not. At first that knowledge, a strange and nagging instinct, telling her (in her mother's voice…) to resist, to pull away and say that this was not what she wanted, disturbed her, but she quickly pushed the thoughts away, sure now that this was, in fact, what she desired, intensely so, and she had known it all along.

She felt his tongue, muscular and well-practised, push her lips apart, as she sighed at the pleasure of the sensation, felt it penetrating her mouth, lapping skilfully and sensually at hers, encouraging her to explore his mouth and tongue with hers. He cradled the back of her head and pulled her towards him, so that her bosom was pressed against his breastbone, and she could sense their two hearts beating in unison. His breathing was as uneven as hers, and the thought that she could raise such a reaction in a man like this excited her.

His hands were assertive, she was quite taken along by them, and as his hands held the back of her head, they tangled in her hair pulling and tugging her to him harder. Rather than feel pain or dread at this however, it caused a thrill to run through her entire body, and she could feel the quaking anticipation right in the centre of her, hot, wet and shaking as it had been on that ride only a short week before. Today those feelings were stronger, the warmth and quivering sensitivity spreading through her whole body from the points where his hands touched her.

A thought surfaced momentarily, through the haze of sensation, that this was so soon after they had met, she should not be feeling like this, behaving like this, quite willingly being seduced by him, in the grounds of his estate! Yet it felt right. She started to think about the wonders of the heart, the mysteries of what makes one person more desirable than another, but she was too distracted by the Earl's burst of passion, and the sensations of his hands on her body, to really focus on anything else.

Their teeth touched as their tongues swirled together, and his lips melded to hers with bruising passion. She found his forcefulness strangely arousing, the intensity of his need for her astonishing. He pulled back a little for a moment, as if he was going to stop, and she instinctively slid her arms around him, pulling him back towards her. With a groan he returned to kissing her, whatever hesitation he had felt gone, in the face of her response.

One hand slid over her neck, then her shoulder, tracing the soft shape of her, drifting down to caress her breast, to brush her hardened nipple through the thin fabric of her dress. Catherine gasped at the sensation, at the burst of pleasure that ran through her, as his fingers teased at her flesh.

Moments later, he took her hand and pressed it firmly against his manhood which she could feel now, hard and throbbing, upright like the oak tree that concealed their tryst from any prying eyes. She was shocked, for she had never touched a man so intimately as this, but she was also excited and aroused – this seemed the most natural thing in the world at this moment, and all thought of consequences had fled her mind.

Before conscious thought could intervene, he lowered her to the ground beside the bench.

He was firmly on top of her, almost pinning her down with his mighty arms like a leopard trapping its prey. Catherine arched her body into his, finding herself even further aroused by his forcefulness – the sensations confused her, but were so wonderful that she wanted more. She grasped him to her, running her hands over him, her fingernails scratching lightly over his skin, where his open shirt gave her access to touch. He kissed her lips, and kissed and nibbled at her neck, and down to the soft rounded tops of her breasts. There was almost something of wild animals to them, biting and scratching at each other on the green summer grass.

His fingers slid under the neckline of her bodice, encountering her hardened nipples, lightly pinching and brushing them, making her arch and squirm in his arms, panting and moaning. She had never thought that her breasts could feel this way!

At the same time, she felt his hand making its way forcefully under her petticoats, towards her inviolate womanhood - she did not resist, in fact she willed him further on, guiding his hand with another arch of her body against him. His touch on her legs trailed higher, and her breath hitched as the amazing sensations flowed through her.

She deepened the kiss in response. Without a moment's warning he was there, touching her most intimate place, rubbing and drawing tiny tactile circles with his fingers, building her moist anticipation up into frantic, feverish gasps.

A passing thought – her mother was right – she had had no idea at all about what this could do to her!

He kept on kissing her, but she could no longer kiss back, she was panting uncontrollably, her breath forced out of her, enraptured by his motions. He nibbled, licked and sucked at her neck and she felt him slide a finger inside her, working it gently as she gasped at the astonishing sensation. He moaned against her neck, but was obviously trying hard to hold back, to ensure her pleasure. Another finger joined the first, and his thumb moved outside her, over that one spot that caused waves of intense sensation to flow through her.

"Catherine," he groaned her name.

She gasped, undone by the need in his voice, and arched up hard against his hand, as pleasure slammed through her, beyond anything that she could have expected. Moments later, as his clever fingers continued their work, she felt the sensations building again, and found herself crying out.

"Charles, please, oh please, I need….."

She had no idea what it was that she needed, she realised, except that he could give it to her.

She felt him move, lift her skirts higher, and ease his weight back off her a moment – she felt oddly bereft without his weight against her, but, before she had time to protest, he was back, his fingers sliding out of her, and suddenly replaced by the feel of his manhood at her entrance.

She froze for one second, but his hand returned, slid between them, working away at her most sensitive spot, and she arched against him, pushing her hips up, seeking the completion that she needed. It was too much for him to stand – any hope of going slowly was gone, and he thrust himself into her, meeting her need with his. Her eyes flew open, and her body contracted around him, as the sharp pain of his entry touched her. He leaned down and kissed her, beginning to move very gently inside her, and the pain slipped away, replaced by new sensations that excited and tantalised, promising ever greater pleasures. She felt him moving inside her and knew that the long vigilance of protecting her virginity was over.

She did not care. This was all too brilliant, too intoxicating to bother with any of that. The Earl, her Charles, moved above her, in her, thrusting harder as he took his pleasure, and it was all she could do not to scream in delight. She felt the impending approach of that ecstasy again as he held himself closer and tighter to her than she had ever been held before.

They shared each other's bodies and flowed into one another gladly, their cries from the pleasure of it all filling each other's ears. Then, with a sudden intense groan Charles thrust hard into her, and stilled. He was spent, He let his weight fall onto her with a sigh, and she trailed her fingers over his back as he lay there, enjoying just being able to touch him, feeling his body still in hers.

After a moment, he rolled over to the side, sliding out of her, easing his weight off her, and tucked his manhood back into his breeches. Catherine lay there for a moment, wide open, skirt still pulled aside, feeling warm and whole, but already yearning for him to touch her again. She stared into the sky and felt that it was entirely within her reach.

"I can only hope that experience was as pleasant for you as for me? I am sorry if I was somewhat... Forceful in my actions, but... you have aroused my passions so much..."

Charles spoke, still breathing unevenly.

"Oh yes, my Lord, that was.... most agreeable," her voice was dazed.

She felt immediately that she should have found better words to express the enormity of what she felt, of the whole new world that had just now opened up before her.

~~~~~

Charles looked at Catherine, still lying on the grass before him, in a state of relaxed abandon, and his heart constricted painfully in his chest.

Guilt overwhelmed him, and a sense of despair.

He was silent, yet inside his thoughts he was raging at himself.

*'What have I done? I am now more than a fool, I am a worse rake then ever I was before! For all my grand resolutions to not diminish Catherine's honour, to not treat her as I did Lady Blanchette, here I am, guilty of doing exactly that.'*

*'At least,'* he thought, with a slight ironic smile, *'I did, this time, have the consideration to bring the lady to pleasure, before reaching my own.'*

That, he had to allow, might also have been because the lady in question was so responsive, so passionate in return, that it had been easy to pleasure her.
~~~~~

He still wanted this woman, wanted to know her better, to have the chance to know her body, over and over, not just in a hurried tryst in the gardens like this.

The despair settled over him – no matter what he wanted, no matter what self-recrimination he indulged in, he had no choice but to marry Blanchette, for he had given his word.

Duty was a terrible cross to bear.

He had no idea how he would ever make reparation to Catherine for what he had just done, in the foolish throes of passion, but the least that he could do was to tell her the truth, now, before his courage failed him.

He looked at her again. She was watching him, her passion hazed eyes half lidded, her expression dreamy, her intense blue eyes darkened. He was about to hurt her desperately, he knew it, yet there was no other choice. Taking a deep breath, he choked back his feelings for her, and spoke.

~~~~~

"Good. I am glad that, for this moment, I could make you happy. Because now I am afraid I have a most regrettable confession to make."

She sat up suddenly. Much of her giddy pleasure subsided at his newly serious tone. She was confused and puzzled – he had gone from passionate and powerful, to hesitant and serious, almost unhappy, looking so fast. She could not imagine what he might be about to say. He was frowning for the first time in their acquaintance, and looking not at her, but off into the distance, back towards the house.
~~~~~

Sitting up, carefully rearranging her clothes, and smoothing her skirts, she studied his serious face.

"Pray tell sir. I am sure that I am quite capable of receiving your confession, whatever it may be."

She did everything she could to sound confident and firm, but she could feel a new dread coming over her.

"There is no easy way to tell you this. My actions have been reprehensible, no matter how strong my passionate care for you may be. I regret to inform you Catherine, in light of what we have just shared, that I am engaged to be married."

"What?! To whom?"

Her voice rose uncontrollably as she spoke, her first reaction one of horror, and of denial that he might be speaking the truth.

Who was this man?

Were all the rumours about him true?

Should she have trusted more to her mother's vague warnings?

She realised, in a wave of shame, that she had not thought beyond the moment at all, that she had wantonly allowed her passion for this man to overcome all of her good sense.

It would seem that her mother had been, lamentably, correct.

"To Lady Blanchette Cavendish, daughter of the Earl of Derbyshire."

Catherine was plunged into a state of shock.

This was all too much!

He had used her, abused her, had his sordid way with her and now he was off, to marry a fellow member of the nobility and leave her to take care of his little niece, as if nothing had happened between them!

It was all just too awful.

She had a sudden urge to be sick.

Every last touch of dreamy pleasure left her body in a rush, as if she had, again, been plunged into the icy cold water of the stream.

"I am deeply sorry Catherine. I am profoundly fond of you, and I hope that we can remain friends. I had never intended, never expected, what is between us to come to this, so fast. But around you... I can't seem to help myself – I wanted you so very badly, and I believed you to feel the same."

"Friends? Sir, I am appalled! To speak of friendship at such a time, really! Your conduct is truly low, beyond all realms of caddishness! When were you planning to tell me this, pray?"

"I'd hoped to inform you as soon as I could, but..."

"As soon as you could?" she interrupted him, too aghast and angry to respect his higher status as her employer and as an aristocrat. "But only after you'd had your way with me, is that so? Take what you want from me and then leave me here in disgrace so as you can marry someone better?"

"It isn't like that Catherine, believe me! I had no say in the matter, if it were up to me I would not be marrying her at all. As I say, I am extremely fond of you, but I'm afraid my family is set upon a suitable match to a Lady from a noble house. I fought this match for years, but, it has been formally agreed – I am duty bound to marry her."

Catherine felt as if he had punched her in the gut.

It was all too horrible.

"I understand. A penniless schoolmistress from the disgraced de Quincey family isn't good enough for the esteemed Earl of Stanningfield. I understand, my Lord. But you will likewise understand if I have developed a strong and sudden urge never to speak to you again."

With that, tears gushing down her face, still hot and red from their moment of passion, she hitched up her skirts and ran back into the house to cry out all her shame and regret, leaving him no opportunity to say anything further.

~~~~~

Charles watched her go, his face a picture of anguish.

If he was honest with himself, he had to admit that his feelings for this woman had grown, at a rate which shocked him.

He wished, with everything in him, that he had never agreed to marry Lady Blanchette.

But he had.

His life seemed to suggest to him that he only ever hurt any woman that he actually cared for.

It was a depressing realisation.

He would find a way to continue around Catherine, without his feelings for her intruding – for Theodora's sake, if nothing else.
~~~~~

He could only hope that, with time, she might forgive him.

The thought brought him no comfort, and the prospect of the long years ahead, in a marriage to a woman that he did not particularly care for, seemed darker and emptier than ever.

For several days Catherine did little but tutor Theodora and cry.

She would wake in the morning, prepare herself a simple breakfast of brown bread and milk, in the pantry, and set about convincing her employer's niece that reading and study were worthwhile pursuits.

Try as she might, she could never quite seem to connect with the girl on the subject of learning, although she found her very pleasant to deal with as soon as they moved their activity or conversation away from the schoolroom.

She was rather disappointed that, when it came to languages and literature, Theodora remained stubborn and headstrong.

Catherine had wanted so desperately to learn, as a girl, and books had been impossible to afford in so many cases, that she struggled to imagine being surrounded by them, and not wanting to learn.

"I simply cannot see the purpose of this book." Theodora declared, when they set about trying to read *Robinson Crusoe*, a novel that Catherine had naively thought would be exciting and modern enough to hold Theodora's attention. "Nothing that is described in it actually took place did it?"

"Well, no, I suppose it is unquestionably a work of fiction." Catherine replied, weary after having repeated a similar routine for days. In some ways, this one girl was more work than the entirety of Harteston Parish School. "But it is based on real events and experiences, and it can tell us a lot of truth about what it means to be human, even if the characters and events are not real."

"I don't understand what you mean," Theodora implored her. "If it isn't real, what truth can there possibly be within it?"

The effort was tiring and demoralised her yet more. It seemed that the Earl was gone, she knew not where, and she certainly was not going to ask.

She told herself that she was glad of it, that it was for the best, that she would simply get on with her life.

But her heart and mind were not so co-operative – she found herself listening for his steps in the hall, and desperately hoping to see him.At the end of each hopeless day, Catherine would head once more to the pantry, there to collect a simple meal which she would generally eat on her own. Cook left out bread, cheese, some cold meats and perhaps some soup or pie for her, and she would simply help herself.

The servants considered themselves distinct from her, despite the fact that they were all live-in employees of the Earl, and stuck to their own already formed circles and cliques.

On one occasion, Catherine had tried to engage Mrs. Cartwright, the housekeeper, or Polly, the doughty woman who had served her tea on her first day at Havisham Hall, in conversation, but the prickly old servants were remarkably dismissive of her efforts.

"Nice to see you Mrs. Cartwright," she had said, warmly.

"And you likewise, Miss," she had said in a haughty tone, before simply carrying on her allotted rounds and ignoring Catherine entirely.

Often she did not even look her in the eye, and Catherine soon gave up on even exchanging pleasantries with her.

She did manage to make one friend, however.

There was a young maid called Anna, who she would often see down in the pantry, loitering without any apparent purpose.

After some time, Catherine decided that it was best to ask her what she was doing down there, after all of the other servants had departed.

"Oh, nothing Miss." Anna spoke somewhat defensively. "Just, er, looking out for mice, that's all. Don't want them running all over the place getting at the grain or the flour now, do we?"

"A worthy endeavour I suppose," Catherine replied, suspiciously. "But it seems a strange time to be going about it. Do you not have any traps, or some poison you could lay down to save yourself the effort of stalking them at all hours?"

"Ah, yes, I see you've got me there Miss. Yes, you're right; doesn't make a whole lot of sense really, me doing that, does it?"

The maid stood in the pantry door, grinning apologetically, and Catherine could not help but feel a small sense of warmth and affection towards this girl.

At least she was willing to talk to her!

She could not have been much younger than her, and had a kind face, pretty in its own way, with pronounced dimples on the cheeks and freckles.

Her thick dark red hair was held back by her maid's headpiece, and she wore the uniform of a serving girl lightly, as if it did not quite suit her to be in so lowly a position within the hierarchy of the house.

Catherine felt a kind of kinship with her, instinctively, she knew that here was another woman who had lived her life with very little, yet had some pride and confidence, and had made the best of what she had.

"What I was actually doing – it's Miss Thornberry, isn't it?" Catherine nodded "...was hanging about here hoping to speak to you. See, we all know how the Earl has treated you. Now don't you ask me how or why, we just know, that's all, been working here more than long enough to know what's what, that's all I'll say."

Catherine was startled – she had not thought that the servants might be aware of her foolishness, or her disgrace.

She flushed with embarrassment and shame, at the thought that they all knew. Anna went on, the words coming in a rush:

"I'd just like to say that I think it's a disgrace, what he's done. You've been really very brave carrying on the way you have in the education of young Theodora, in the light of all that's happened, and I, for one, am just about brim-full of respect for you. Brim-full. I'm sorry if any of the other staff have been a bit unfriendly with you as well, they don't mean anything by it, it's just their way with strangers, see. Most of them share my high opinion of you, at least those that haven't been here for so long that they'll just support his lordship and never question him no matter what. Well anyway, I've talked plenty now, but I just wanted to say, you do have at least one friend here at Havisham Hall."

Anna beamed a big grin at her, slightly embarrassed to have said so much, all in one go, but sincere in her expression of friendship. Catherine was full of gratitude for this kindness.

"Thank you Anna. That's very nice to hear."

"In any case, I'll let you finish your supper, but just so you know, should there be anything you require, anything at all, just ask, and I shall do my best to assist you in whatever way I can."

"You are too kind. Thank you again."

After finishing her soup, Catherine retired, as she did every day, to her quarters. The quiet isolation gave her space to think, to not have to keep on pretending that everything was normal.

Unlike the grandeur of the main part of the house with its elegant drawing rooms and sumptuous decoration, her two rooms, which she had been shown to by the housekeeper on that first night, were in the servants' quarters, and were therefore very plain and simple.

Admittedly, they were in the better part of the servants quarters, on the same higher floor of the building as Theodora's suite of rooms, with a lovely view out over the gardens from the small window, but still, they were plain. Somehow she had not yet found a way to add anything to make them feel more homely. She had a small bed, serviceable enough but not anyone's idea of especially comfortable, and, in her tiny sitting room, a bare, unvarnished desk, the wood of which had chipped away over the years, and which gave her splinters if she ever tried to write on it.

There was a modest, single shelf attached to the left wall adjacent to her bed, where she had put the few books that she had, and a little cabinet in the desk, as well as one small closet where she could store her clothes. The walls were whitewashed and cracked, with much of the paintwork, which had probably been applied decades ago, at least, flaking away.

There was a slight smell of lingering damp throughout the room, which she had noticed had started to get into her hair and clothes, an indignity she had not expected to suffer on moving to a grand and stately home.

Perhaps the rooms had been empty, for a long while before she came to them.

She was grateful for the small window on the back wall, with its pleasant view of the grounds at the back of the house, but it let in so little light by late in the day, that she was often forced to light up the precious supply of candles that she was afforded, to have light enough to read by. The boards of the bare wooden floor would creak as she picked her way back into her room of an evening, to read and re-read the novels she had with her, or compose letters in which she falsely reassured her mother that she was happy and that all was well.

She was just sitting down to write such a letter, pen inches above the ink-well, when an unexpected knock at the door made her jump, it being so unlikely that anyone would seek her out here. Startled for a moment, she placed the pen back down and went to the door. She was utterly shocked, upon opening the door, to see her employer, the Earl, standing in front of her, wearing his crimson smoking jacket and looking far more nervous, indeed almost sheepish, than usual. Despite her decision that she never wanted to see, or speak to him again, she found her traitorous heart beating faster, and a sensation suspiciously like happiness rising inside her. She repressed it firmly.

"I hope I am not disturbing you," he said immediately, in a subdued tone.

Despite everything that had happened between them, or perhaps because of it, she still felt a flutter in her stomach, and a growing warmth in her intimate places, at the sight of him – her body remembered the pleasure, even if her mind was focussed on the hurtfulness of his actions.

"My Lord! This is most unexpected. No, I suppose you are not disturbing me." She tried as hard as she could not to be rude or churlish towards him. He was still paying her a wage after all, and a more generous one than it needed to be, at that. And, in the end, no matter how frustrating the girl was, she did like Theodora, and did not want to leave, and doom her to a cranky and unforgiving governess in the traditional mould. "What, pray, brings you to my humble quarters at this hour?"

Her voice was hard, all of her repressed hurt hidden just under the surface of her words.

"Please Catherine..."

He moved into her room without her permission, as he spoke.

The house was his property, but she baulked slightly at this sudden invasion of her little corner of privacy.

"I wish you wouldn't speak to me in that tone – it is terrible to hear such coldness in your voice. I wanted to come and see you, to express my profoundest regret at how I behaved, and at having betrayed you as I have."

"Some, sir, would say that your apology is long overdue."

"Yes, I can see that you would perceive it like that. I've had to go away, this past few days, to finalise arrangements for this accursed wedding. Had I been here, I would have redoubled my efforts to demonstrate my regret to you, at every opportunity. Can you forgive me?"

She looked him straight in his dark, compelling eyes. He looked sincere in his intentions - indeed Catherine almost thought that he looked genuinely distressed. It had been decent of him to come to her like this.

Although, his mention of the wedding made her feelings of hurt all the sharper again.

"I can sir, but with a heavy heart. You have stripped me of my innocence, and my honour, and deceived me quite deliberately. I trust that our relationship will heal, but it will take time - time that I am only willing to grant you for Theodora's sake."

"Oh Catherine!" he said, plucking her hand from her side and holding it against his breast for a moment. He pressed a kiss to the sensitive flesh of her palm quickly, and let out a great sigh of relief.

"My heart swells with affection for you, I cannot thank you enough. Believe me when I tell you, my very soul has been swallowed by guilt these past few days. I wish I did not have to marry Lady Blanchette, with all my heart, but alas, a gentleman of my station must consider his duty to his house and successors. And I have given my word on it, some time ago – it would bring her great dishonour should I cry off at this late stage. I had never expected to meet someone else, someone who affected me as you do."

Her skin tingled where his lips had pressed, and a warmth spread through her, her nipples tightening in response. No matter what she thought, her body had very distinct opinions about his closeness.

"Thank you for your candour, sir, and I am pleased that you regret your actions. Now however, I should like some peace and quiet in which to write my letters, and then the space required for a good night's sleep."

He looked pained at her cold response. A tiny, guilty part of her was glad that she could still wound the heart of a man like the Earl. Perhaps their relationship was not quite as broken as she had initially thought – if he could seem to be so wounded by her words, could it be that he told the truth, when he spoke of his affection for her? That thought raised a tiny flutter in her heart, a little piece of hope. A hope that she fiercely repressed, by reminding herself that he was to wed another, that, no matter her feelings or his, there was nothing here for her.

"Of course!" he said humbly. "How tactless of me, I shall leave you in peace. Only, whatever may have happened between us, and whatever uncertainties the future holds for both our fates, know that you will always occupy a pre-eminent position in my heart."

He paused to plant a solemn kiss on the top her head, smiled weakly, and left at once. Maybe, just maybe, despite his past indiscretions and his lusty habits of life, Charles Rockingham wasn't such a terrible man after all.

112

Charles sat in his study, the scatter of papers, all relating to his upcoming wedding, cluttering his desk.

The organisation, and cost, involved in a wedding was truly horrifying.

He didn't care.

Thank God his mother had chosen to live in the Dower House when his father died. He would have gone mad by now where she here in the house with him.

She was currently wedding obsessed, as the union between Charles and Lady Blanchette was the culmination of 20 years plotting on her part. He would have found it amusing, were he not one of the major characters in this farce.

He could not get Catherine out of his thoughts.

The feeling of utter despair, which had overtaken him when she ran from him in the grounds, had stayed with him all through the last few days as he had visited tailors and dealt with all of the trivia associated with the wedding and managing the alarmingly large influx of guests that was expected. It had only eased this evening, when he had finally managed the courage to go to Catherine and apologise, again.

This time, she had listened long enough for him to ask her forgiveness, and she had been gracious enough to grant it.

But the coldness in her voice had chilled him to the heart, and the uncertainty of her manner towards him made him castigate himself even more, for the utter fool that he was. He knew that passion made him forceful, and could overcome him – why had he put either of them in a position where that could happen? He knew the answer – because he was selfish, because he wanted her, and he had not considered the impact of his actions on her future.

He did not like the answer, but he accepted it.

His thoughts ran round and round, an endless circle going nowhere, and found no answer. In eight days, he would marry. No matter that he did not love, or even care for, the woman he would marry, no matter that he had come to care for Catherine, had come, dare he even think the word, to love her.

There was no way out.

No solution which allowed everyone to be happy, and still be true to honour and duty.

He could not even lose himself in drink, or any other pastime – there was too much to do.

He would have to simply push his feelings aside and immerse himself in the management of the house and the estates, and the preparation for the guests' arrival.

Yet still he sat, ignoring the papers, and stared at nothing, Catherine's face haunting his thoughts. There was only one idea that had come to him, which might, in some way, allow him to have what he wanted. It was a thought that he was ashamed of, yet it came back to him – for surely that would be better than nothing at all?

He pushed the idea aside. It was not right. But it nagged at him. Annoyed, he pushed himself away from the desk and took himself to his chambers. It was late, and there was much to do tomorrow. Perhaps if he rose early and took Thaddeus out for a gallop, he might face the situation with better grace.

~~~~~

And so it went, for the next four days. Charles dragged himself through the day, dealing with interminable preparations, meeting with his mother to deal with everything that she demanded, taking Thaddeus out each morning in an attempt to ride out his frustrations. Catherine haunted his thoughts, and, when he saw her in the house, he ached to draw her to him and hold her. He forced himself to turn away instead, with a polite greeting, and escaped to another part of the house.

On the evening of the fourth day, he sat again in the study, nursing a large brandy, and considered the morrow. In the morning he would ride.
~~~~~

In the afternoon, Lady Blanchette and her family would arrive, as would some other guests, and the major activities would begin. Three days after that, he would be wed. It was still a surreal thought, and it appealed less than it ever had before.

He ached for Catherine. He wanted to touch her, kiss her, hold her, feel her body beneath his. The thought that he might never do so again was unbearable. Yet he must accept that reality. In a sudden fit of frustration, he downed the brandy in one gulp, and smashed the glass on the stones of the hearth. Turning, he took himself to his bed.

# Chapter Fourteen

The next day the house was full of unfamiliar people, and frantic energy, as the Cavendish family arrived from Derbyshire with Lady Blanchette.

With only three days to go until the wedding, there was an enormous amount of preparation to be getting on with.

The kitchens became a hive of activity as the chefs prepared all manner of dishes; stuffed geese, pigeon pie, plum pudding and turtle soup, endless platters of fruits, meats, pickles, and cheeses, and of course, the *piece de resistance*, an immense wedding cake.

The deepest cold cellar was full of prepared items, and more ingredients where delivered continuously.

Catherine could barely move for all of the extra staff taken on for the effort, and was forced to sip her soup and nibble her bread and cheese in a tiny alcove off the pantry, keeping out of their way, lest she be trampled underfoot.

Anna had the unenviable task of helping them to scrub dishes, although that was not part of her normal work, working her way through a seemingly endless cycle of huge copper pots and pans. Cheerful by nature though, she whistled a merry tune and got on with her task.

By contrast, Catherine felt even more morose and heartbroken.

She had seen Charles, in the distance, a couple of time in the day, always surrounded by his new relations to be, looking as handsome as ever, and even more unattainable. She sternly reprimanded herself for caring, but still could not help but look for him everywhere she went.

She had been overwhelmingly shocked when she discovered just how soon his wedding was to happen, with her shock rapidly turning to bitter anger at him, all over again, followed by despair.

If it were not for the need to keep Theodora quietly occupied in the midst of the chaos, she might have simply run from the house and not come back.

But... where would she go? She could not return to her mother, and tell her the terrible truth – her mother would be so disappointed, and would harp at her about it forever after. Anna broke into her gloomy musings with a question.

"How much of this feast do you think will be left over for us?" she asked Catherine with a cheeky grin.

"I reckon about half. These posh types don't tend to eat all that much. They wouldn't be able to squeeze their way into their fancy frocks and coats if they did! I'm not complaining! I can't wait to sink my teeth into a piece of that cake!"

Despite the sadness in her heart, and her deep regret that this wedding, which shamed her by its very proximity, and by stealing from her the man that she had believed that she loved, she laughed along with Anna, and felt a little spark of excitement at the prospect of seeing all of the beautiful clothes and decorations associated with so grand a wedding.

Regardless of anything else, this whole episode in her life was giving her a chance to see inside the lives of the nobility, which she would never have otherwise been able to do.

Before her duties with Theodora began for the day, from her little window at the back of the house, Catherine watched the preparations. The servants were setting up the gardens so that guests feeling too warm in the ballroom would be able to take the air outside, surrounded by beauty, and with refreshments close to hand. Tables and chairs would be laid out throughout the gardens, providing places for guests refresh themselves, should the banquet presented indoors prove inadequate to their needs.

One of the terraces outside the French windows from the house had been set up as a stand for an orchestra to regale the guests outdoors with music, in addition to the musicians engaged in the ballroom where those so inclined would enjoy themselves dancing.

She had to confess to herself that it was all very exhilarating, the prospect of all of these grand celebrations, and the presence of so many of England's wealthiest and most important people, here to celebrate love and marriage.

Well, she corrected herself, marriage anyway – there was not much of love associated with most wedding in the *ton*.

She only regretted that all of this decoration, and the enormous feast being prepared down below was not for her wedding to Charles, but for that of another, a Lady with a real title and more money than she could ever dream of, rather than a penniless governess with nothing but a pretty face, a certain cleverness, and an old link to an ancient family to recommend her.

She did not even see Lady Blanchette until the next day when the Earl formally presented his household to his bride to be.

They were, after all, to be her servants as well as his, once the match was complete, and he thought it prudent to introduce them now.

They all lined up in the entrance foyer of Havisham Hall, in their finest livery, from the butler and the steward, right down to the junior groundskeeper and scullery maid, as Lady Blanchette, her father Lord Derbyshire, and the Earl passed along the line.

Lady Blanchette was undeniably pretty. She had a small, heart-shaped face that was dainty and well-proportioned, with pert lips and piercing blue eyes the shape of almonds. Her dark glossy hair was beautifully dressed.

She wore a sumptuous dress, in red and black, which accentuated her womanly figure, curved at the hips, and, though she was not a tall woman, she had a certain gravitas that Catherine presumed came from the inevitable effect of her breeding and of the authority that is automatically granted to those of the aristocracy.

Each of the servants bowed or curtsied to her, without her saying more than a few words to them.

Lord Derbyshire, who seemed to be rather old and wore his thin grey hair in an old-fashioned manner, appeared bored by the entire exercise, dawdling at the rear with his hands behind his back. He appeared to be focusing more on the family paintings of past and present Earls of Stanningfield, than on the staff of Havisham Hall.

However, when the party got to Catherine, who was standing near the end of the line, wearing her best green dress, Lady Blanchette thought to say a little more than usual:

"And you must be the governess?" she said immediately, in a voice as clear and crisp as a mountain spring.

"Yes, my lady." Catherine responded as demurely as she dared. "Catherine Thornberry is my name."

"And a charming name it is too!" Lady Blanchette said, somewhat too brightly. Catherine was unsure what to make of her manner. Did she know about what she and Charles had done under the oak tree? Surely not. "Charles has told me all about you. He says you are the cleverest young lady in all of Suffolk, and one of the prettiest besides. I can see that he was not exaggerating in his praise."

"You are too generous, Lady Blanchette." Catherine said, curtseying awkwardly.

"I will be most honoured to have you as a member of our household. I am sure that, with your attentions focussed completely on Theodora, she will learn, and not be a nuisance to us at all."

Blanchette fixed Catherine with a steely gaze.

Though her mouth formed a smile, Catherine sensed a certain coldness in her bearing, the smile did not reach her eyes. The sentiment expressed by her words did not appeal – Theodora did not deserve to be shut away from the Earl, and from the other activities of the house. Catherine saw a momentary expression of displeasure cross Charles' face, where he stood beside Lady Blanchette, then it was gone.

She mumbled in reply.

"Thank you my lady. I am deeply honoured."

And the Earl's bride-to-be passed on down the line.

Catherine's eyes met Charles' as he passed, and she noticed him throw her a wry little smile. She had to bite the inside of her lip to prevent herself from smiling too broadly in response. Instead, she chose a stern and disapproving expression, hoping that it would make him at least a little sad.

That night Catherine lay awake in bed, writing in her diary and pondering Lady Blanchette's words and actions.

She was unsure what to make of them, and had little experience of high society, or the whims of beautiful, powerful young noblewomen, to draw on. The idea of recording her thoughts and feelings from this strange period of her life had come to her a few days before, and now she set about it, scribbling notes to herself in an empty journal, by candlelight.

She had settled to a sort of sleepy peacefulness, finally starting to accept that there was nothing that she could do – he would marry another, no matter how much her heart ached, when, with a suddenness that caused her to sit up and gasp, the Earl burst into her room, without any sort of a knock or any kind of prior warning.

She instinctively recoiled in fear, but when she realised who it was her heart leapt in foolish hope and she felt a crazy urge to smile and laugh.

"My Lord!" she said, her breathing suddenly hurried and uneven, "...why, what on earth are you doing here?"

"Hush, my Catherine."

He turned to close the door and drew his finger to his lips to command her to be quiet.

At this show of authority, she stilled and sank back deeper into her bed, shutting the diary and placing it on the floor as she did so. Suddenly realising that she wore only her night rail, she drew the covers up to her shoulders, feeling vulnerable and unsure.

Charles came further into the room, tip-toed over the creaky floorboards and perched himself on the edge of her bed with a rapid, smooth movement, as if he'd practised this before. In the dim light of her small candle, he looked as handsome as ever. She could make out the edges of his jawline and his high, well-crafted cheekbones.

As before, she felt an urge to reach out and touch his face, to trace his jaw.

"I just wanted to say Catherine," he began, gazing at her passionately "–that, though I may be obliged to marry Lady Blanchette in a mere two days' time, my thoughts have been constantly of you. I cannot stop my mind from returning to thoughts of you, again and again, and I do not believe that any woman has ever had such a profound effect upon me before. As strange as it may be to say it, at a time such as this, I think I love you, Catherine Thornberry."

Catherine sat up.

She was, of course, surprised, and deeply flattered, happy beyond words and despairing at the same time, filled with great sadness and anger. She could feel the same shaking in her bosom and quivering sensation in her body, and especially between her legs, that Charles Rockingham had always caused in her.

Now she knew that those feelings were wanton desire, it made no difference – she found that she craved his touch, even whilst she hated their situation.

She had hoped, had in some way, already sensed that this was what he felt. There was a connection between them, some force that seemed to be drawing them together. A force strong enough that it overcame her anger, overcame her resolution to be sensible, and made her want simply to be in his arms.

No matter how set in stone his dynastic marriage into the Cavendish family might be, she had come to realise that nothing could change the feelings that they shared.

Which only made the situation all the more painful and impossible.

"I know," she said. "-and I care about you very deeply, nay, I love you, as well, Charles Rockingham. You may be a cad, but you are also the most wonderful man that I have ever had the privilege of knowing – but...."

Before she could finish her sentence he had grabbed her, and was kissing her passionately, frantically holding her body close to his. The angry words that she had been about to say were swallowed by his kiss and all thought of them slid from her mind, as the onslaught of sensation from her body took over.

The same warm and powerful sensations, which she had felt under the tree on the grounds, overcame her, and she surrendered herself to him. It was delicious, it was everything she dreamed of, she felt safe and desired in his arms, even when she knew that none of this could possibly be.

Still kissing her, he pulled the bedcovers away from her body, stilling her protest with another kiss, trailing kisses from her mouth, down her neck, across her collar bone and down the upper slope of her breasts, as his deft fingers undid the ties of her nightrail and pushed it aside to allow him access to her nipples.

Her fingers tangled in his hair, holding him to her, as she gasped and arched up to him when his warm mouth and clever tongue found the hard peak of her breast and proceeded to lick, suck and nibble on it, creating sensations in her body that she had never imagined possible.

Sensations more intense even than those she had felt when he had taken her in the grounds, sensations that she wanted to explore, to feel more and more of.

Continuing his loving treatment of her breasts, suckling one and then the other, one hand supporting his weight above her, his other hand reached down and slowly drew up the hem of her nightrail, trailing his touch up the silken softness of the skin of her inner thigh as he did so.

She was squirming, arching her body against him, feeling heat building within her, and moisture gathering between her legs, in that most intimate place.

Her breathing was ragged, and she found herself helplessly calling his name then making little mewling noises as her body was flooded with sensation.

He slid up to kiss her mouth again, and her breasts ached for him to return to them, until that sensation was overridden by the next, as his fingers slid inside her, and began to work at bringing her to a peak of pleasure. He moaned aloud as he touched her moist folds, finding her so very wet and ready for him, and the sound and feeling of his moan against her lips aroused her even further.

She felt that she had no control whatsoever over her, oh, so wanton, body, and her hips rose to meet the thrusts of his fingers, as she felt the irresistible wave of pleasure grow within her.

It was amazing, it was wonderful, she wanted more, needed more, even though, at the same time, it was so strong a sensation as to be unbearable. Helplessly, she found herself at the peak of pleasure, and falling, falling, over it, into an indescribable and wonderful place.

As she fell, she felt his fingers leave her, and instantly missed the warmth of the intimate connection. Moments later, as she reached for him, pleading wordlessly, he came back to her, and slid his deliciously hard cock inside her.

It was slower than the time on the grounds, and she revelled in the sensation of being filled, of no pain whatsoever, only a delicious sense of fullness, and of sensitive nerve endings being stroked by his every movement.

Charles kept his movements slow, and deliberate, the effort obviously costing him much concentration, but when Catherine reached up, sliding her hands under his loose hanging shirt, and gliding them over the sculpted muscle of his body, he lost all hope of control, and began to thrust into her, feverishly, hard and fast, bending his head to gently bite at her nipples or lick and suck them.

She clutched him to her, her body contracting around his, and found herself about to come again, about to fall into ecstasy.

She cried out as she came, and the sight, sound and feel of her tipped Charles over the edge too. They collapsed into each other's arms, to lie still, and sated, and both pretending desperately that tomorrow did not exist.

But tomorrow did exist.

After a short while, Charles gently disentangled himself from her, and sighing, put his clothes to rights.

"Oh my Catherine, I love you, but I am still honour bound to leave you. I see no way out, and that leaves me feeling dark despair. I want you desperately, but I must marry another. Perhaps... would you consider... Could I possibly ask it of you... would you be willing to be my mistress?"

Catherine looked at him, suddenly feeling cold and abandoned, all of the beautiful, warm afterglow of their lovemaking blown away by the icy wind of his question.

She was hurt, shocked, and offended, and spent no time considering it, before snapping out her reply.

"No!" and turning away from him. Charles reached out a hand to touch her, but she pushed him away. "Leave me alone!"

She near shouted the demand, turning from him and pulling the covers over her head.

She felt the bed shift, heard him move, hesitate, then sighing, leave the room. She waited until she heard the door click shut, and his steps recede down the corridor, before letting herself indulge in tears of wracking grief.

Leaving an equally miserable Charles, with no choice but to steal off back into the night, returning to the life that he was duty-bound to lead, elsewhere, away from her.

# Chapter Fifteen

The day before the wedding, Catherine took a day's leave and went back to her mother's cottage in Harteston. It was not a difficult decision to make, the house had become so consumed with pre-wedding activity that she could barely sleep, let alone find a moment's peace or privacy during the day.

Theodora was to have a part in the wedding, as an attendant, and had been excited by all of the fuss, by the more adult styled new gown that had been made for her, and by the increasing scale of the preparations. She had been more distracted than ever before, speaking constantly of the impending marriage rather than focussing on her learning. This had, quite predictably, made Catherine's task an impossibility, and so she had taken the liberty of writing a note to her employer:

*My Lord Stanningfield,*

*I regret that it has become necessary for me to temporarily quit Havisham Hall for Harteston. My mother has taken ill, and I am required by her bedside at once. I offer my sincere apologies for any disruption to the affairs of your household, or to Mistress Theodora's education.*

*Yours faithfully,*

*Miss Catherine Thornberry*

It was a brief and blunt letter, but she expected him to understand. The fact that her mother was not really ill, caused her a twinge of guilt as she wrote, but she felt that she needed some unquestionable reason for her actions. The very thought of him and of their intimacy drove her to distraction, and she was tormented many times a day by reminders of his betrothal to another. Equally distracting was the idea that he could even consider asking her to be his mistress – did that mean that he really did love her, and could not bear to lose her? Or did it mean that he really did not love her, and was merely looking for a relationship of physical convenience?

She was so very confused. Sitting in the middle of the preparations for a wedding that was not for her, between the man she loved and a woman she could not warm to, was simply too much to bear. She resolved to spend the next few days back in the village, away from this strange form of torture until after the wedding was over.

Without lapsing into painful or unseemly levels of detail, Catherine told her mother about the situation in which she found herself. She had expected Mother Thornberry to be angry with her, and to insist that she had made a mistake, but she was more compassionate than she had expected.

"Well, as they always say, the course of true love never did run smooth," she said, hugging her daughter close, with warmth and affection.

The stew pot was in its usual place over the fire, filled with a rich smelling stew that had obviously benefitted from the food sent by the Earl. Catherine's single bed was warm and freshly made, and outside, the Forget-me-nots were emitting their sweet scent. Everything seemed to be in its right and proper place.

"Oh mother," Catherine whimpered. "How can I bear it? I feel as if my heart could only ever beat for him, and yet he is to marry another. I fear that I will be forever sad and alone."

"Don't talk such rubbish child!" her mother replied at once, patting her cheek to make her point more forcefully.

"Even if this rather unfortunate situation does not play out as you desire, well, there are plenty of other handsome young gentleman out beyond the four walls of this cottage, who would be inclined to take a shine to a pretty and clever young Miss like yourself. If you can attract the affections of one man such as the Earl of Stanningfield, why then should you presume that you could not catch the eye of another?"

"But mother, I may never meet such a man as him again, in all my life! And I would want a man such as him, a man that I could love." she exclaimed, with a hint of desperation in her voice.

"It is not every day that one is saved from drowning in a stream ten minutes' walk from one's own house by a handsome young Earl! You speak as if every man in the kingdom was as good-looking and charming, or as if every other young buck with wild oats to sow had a great name, house, and estate behind him! Occurrences such as these are rare, indeed, I feel I may have drawn out more than my allotted due of good fortune already. And now to see him spurn me and marry another, it is all too much for a fragile heart to bear."

"You forget one thing my dear," said her mother, with a twinkle in her eye. "He has expressed his love for you. His marriage to this Lady Blanchette is taking place against his will, despite her many virtues and excellent pedigree, the result of a contract made when they were mere children, as I understand it. If he was sincere in the expression of his heartfelt desires, then you should not abandon all hope just yet."

"I do not know mother. I cannot stand it. To think of him wed to another for the remainder of his days - for the remainder of my days, to come to think of it – it is enough to make one lose all desire to go on living."

"Don't talk such rot girl! Why if we all simply gave up on things every time we faced a little difficulty, then none of us would be here at all! Had I given up, then you and I most certainly would not be here today. You must hold your head high, take some pride and carry on as you were. There is nothing else for it."

Mother patted her cheek once again, and went back to stirring the old pot.

Charles had not slept – he had lain there and thought of Catherine, feeling lost and achingly sad. Here it was, the day of his wedding, and he still really had no interest in marrying Lady Blanchette.

He desperately wished that he could marry Catherine. He wanted a woman that he loved, not a typical *ton* marriage. He wanted a woman who could care for Theodora, even though she was stubborn and strong minded, not a woman who saw her as an inconvenience.

He wanted, most importantly, a woman who loved him, with whom he could share passion, not a woman who simply submitted to him because she had to, as his wife.

There was still no solution that would give him all of that.

When Catherine had rejected his suggestion that she become his mistress, he had been happy – for he did not really wish to put her in such as position, where she would be looked down on, and scorned. Yet there was no other way in which he could retain his honour, do his duty and also have Catherine.

Perhaps duty was not so sensible a way of life after all, if it made people so terribly unhappy. Honour he could still see some value in – in fact, in this case, he felt that what he was about to do was distinctly dishonourable, even if it was his duty.

The thought galled him.

Even through his most rakish days, he had still held to honourable behaviour, as much as he could.

'Yes,' said that insidious voice in his mind, *'the last time that you acted in a truly, regrettably dishonourable fashion was Monique – and you vowed not to be like that again….'*

Irritated, with himself and the world, he pushed the thoughts away, and forced himself to rise, ring for Johnson, and prepare for the day.

~~~~~

Against her instincts, and possibly her better judgement, Catherine decided to go along to see the wedding. If pressed on the matter, she would have struggled to immediately explain why. Perhaps it was a desire to firmly close that chapter of her life, and to demonstrate to the Earl and his new bride that she bore no bitterness towards them, in spite of what had happened.
~~~~~

Perhaps part of her genuinely wished Charles Rockingham well, and desired only to express her fondness for him through this gesture of contrition.

She did, most genuinely, regret the way that they had parted, when he came to her room that last time.

But perhaps there was a part of her, some dark instinct for power inherited from the de Quincys, which suspected that everything was not entirely over between herself and the man that she'd presumed to love.

That she still, very much, loved.

After their amazing lovemaking in her quarters, she had surmised that she still, despite the demands of his family, had some power over him, held him still in her sway, although his asking her to be his mistress had shaken that a little. It was impossible to say for certain, but she knew, at least, that she did not feel utterly resigned and miserable as she took the walk along the country roads to St. Jude's Church at Harteston, but rather had a, probably foolish, sense of hope and possibility.

She knew that St. Jude, patron of the parish, was the saint of lost causes, and perhaps this gave her some strange sense of hope.

It was a very attractive church, which she knew well. Two great and ancient yew trees stood over the entrance to the churchyard, marked with a wooden gatehouse painted black. Passing under these, the splendid medieval tower of the church loomed over the visitor, a reminder of the power of the almighty. Its sturdy Gothic stones had been laid down in the late Middle Ages, back when Suffolk's agriculture and the wool trade had made it the wealthiest county in England, with even its most modest parish churches built on a grand scale.

Age-old Gargoyles leered down at her, as they had at visitors to this church for hundreds of years, threatening and promising in equal measure. Atop it all was a weather vane in the shape of the Archangel Michael, warrior-messenger of the heavens. He was leading her, as he had led legions of the faithful in the past, into her very own battle. She smiled at her fanciful thoughts, and turned to the church entry.

She was almost late, and most of the guests had already filed into the pews for the service. Catherine was, by some margin, the most modestly dressed of them all, wearing the same plain grey dress that she had worn the day that Charles had accidentally tipped her into the Shimpling Stream.

It was not an accident that she wore this humble garment, which she knew held great sentimental value for her, and hopefully for today's groom.

Sliding inconspicuously into the very back of the church, she easily avoided the gaze of all the various grandees in their finest frocks and elegant suits.

So many of the gentlemen wore the tall hats that she understood were just coming into fashion in London society, along with bulging complicated white cravats and collars. The ladies, many accompanied by servant attendants, wore corset bodies, covered by bodices of beautiful silks, which seemed tighter than it was possible for any bodice to be, pressing their figures hard into an elegant, curved shape. Their over opulent and spreading skirts made pools of colour in the shaded church.

Though she admired the appearance of them, Catherine was privately glad that she was not smart or wealthy enough to be expected to wear such uncomfortable looking garments. Not clever or wealthy enough yet, anyway.

The organist droned out a few pious bars of music, and the assembled congregation all took their seats. Catherine perched on the end of the rearmost rank of pews beside a formidable older woman, who threw her, and her modest garments, a disbelieving glance before facing the altar. With the guests all seated, she could suddenly see him, her lover, looking more marvellous now that he ever had before, in a superbly tailored black coat with an immense white flower in his button hole. His hair was more buoyant than she had seen it, worn high and thickly curling, as irrepressible as ever.

He stood next to the reedy-faced vicar, mumbling something to a gentleman she presumed must be his brother, based on some similarity in their appearance, who was holding a small box, which likely contained the wedding ring.

What glorious diamonds or other gems might be encrusted on that ring! She allowed herself to fantasize about it slipping, glistening and wonderful, onto her finger. Her eyes met those of the Earl for just a second and she blushingly turned away. He had seen her though, of that she could be certain.

The organ piped up again and Lady Blanchette entered. Catherine had to admit that the woman, who was to break her heart forever, looked glorious in her wedding dress. It was as pure white as freshly-fallen snow, with her glossy dark hair covered by a fine veil that gave the woman's face an air of innocence and piety that it did not, on its own, possess.

She held a fabulous bouquet of hothouse flowers of types that Catherine had never even seen before.

Her dress had such a long train flowing out behind her that it took six attendants, including her young charge Theodora (who looked even more excited than before, if that was possible!), with a ring of flowers around her head.

Theodora, stubbornly herself, grinned as she recognised her governess and Catherine could not help but beam a smile and a subtle wave back.

The bridal party reached the altar, and the organ came to a prompt halt. Catherine could see the Earl whispering something, most likely some compliment, into his betrothed's ear, before the Vicar started up.

"Dearly beloved, in the presence of God, Father, Son and Holy Spirit, we have come together to witness the marriage of Charles Rockingham, Earl of Stanningfield, and Lady Blanchette Cavendish, to pray for God's blessing on them…"

Catherine was too preoccupied with her own thoughts to properly take in the priest's words. He plodded on through the opening prayer and words of welcome, and the wedding guests dutifully listened. She could not see Charles's face from her position at the back of the church, and had no opportunity to surmise how enthusiastic he was feeling about all of this, now that the moment had actually arrived.

"If anyone present knows any reason why these two may not be joined together forever in Holy Matrimony, let him speak now, or else forever hold his peace."

Her heart lurched forward slightly at this familiar, ominous moment. Being careful not to move her head to bring attention to herself, she scanned the room with her eyes.

No-one stirred, no hands were raised. She would not be relieved so easily then. Unexpectedly, Charles had turned around slightly, causing a murmur to run through the church, and once more she felt his gaze fall upon her. Again, she looked down at the floor rather than meet his eyes directly.

She heard the vicar start the vows:

"The vows you are about to take are to be made in the presence of God, who is judge of all and knows all of the secrets of our hearts, therefore, if either of you knows any reason why you may not lawfully marry, you must declare it now."

Silence hung heavy around the church.

The vicar allowed for the customary pause, used to passing over these formalities with nothing happening.

Catherine could just about make out Charles, shifting his weight uncomfortably, at the front of the church.

Nevertheless, it seemed that he would keep his silence, until, suddenly, he cleared his throat and spoke:

"I know a reason."

The vicar took a step backwards in shock.

This was most improper, most unexpected, in fact, completely unheard of at a wedding of the nobility!

He seemed unsure even of what to say in response.

"You do, my Lord?" he said at last, nervously.

"Yes. If, as you say, God knows all of the secrets of our hearts, then I'm afraid he would be rather appalled at mine. I love another, and have lain with her outside the bounds of wedlock. Surely that would be cause for me not to enter this marriage in the eyes of God?"

"Charles!" The Earl's mother stood up in horror from the front row. "What is this madness?"

"Do your duty boy!" said another, possibly an uncle. "This is no time for pious confessions! We're here for a wedding!"

"You may very well be…" said Charles firmly, turning now to face the congregation. Lady Blanchette kept her silence, the veil disguised the expression on her face. "…I however, have no intention of going through with this. I am sorry, Lady Blanchette, but I cannot marry you. I have already given my heart to another, and it would therefore be false of me to take these vows now."

There were cries of outrage throughout the church.

Charles' mother surged to her feet, shrieking.

"Who, pray? Who are you talking about Charles? What the devil has overcome you?"

His mother sank back, almost fainting. The vicar tried to protest this unseemliness in his church, but he was drowned out by the newly raised commotion.

"Catherine Thornberry."

Charles' voice thundered, reaching straight to her, at the back of the church, as he answered his mother's question.

Catherine stood up, and it was all she could do not to cry out in delight, though she felt rather faint and shaky with shock.

Her heart beat so hard that she shook with it, and her breathing came short. He had declared her shame to everyone here, and she did not care, for he had also declared his love for her.

Could this really be happening, and to her?

Such drama!

Her heart overflowed with joy, and she was filled with a desire to sing.

"She has quite overcome me, and I have loved her since the very first time I saw her," he was walking towards her, striding purposefully down the aisle of the church. She clapped her hands to her face in shock. All eyes were upon her now, some scowling, some simply confused, but a few of the old-fashioned romantics present seemed to be smiling. The old woman sitting next to her gave her a quiet nod of appreciation. "Those of you who have come here to witness a staid and predictable dynastic marriage may be disappointed," he declared to the assembled throng "-but I freely admit that I care not."

Now he was before her, dropping down onto his knee. He did not have a ring on his person, so he simply held out his hands as a gesture of devotion to her.

"Catherine Thornberry, would you be my bride?"

She gasped audibly.

Everyone there, Lords and Ladies, members of wealthy and powerful families, grandees who had come to see an exchange of vows and property between grand old families, all craned their necks at her in expectation. There was a sense that the entire church full of people held its collective breath.

She could not have said anything other than:

"Yes. Yes of course, I'll marry you!"

With that, Charles Rockingham rose to his feet and, in one powerful sweep, gathered her up in his arms and kissed her with a passion the like of which many watching in that church had never even seen, let alone felt. Cradling her close in his strong embrace, he turned and carried her towards the altar, to stand before the vicar expectantly.

Lady Blanchette drew herself up stiffly, and with a repressed hiss of anger, turned and strode from the church, followed by her closest family. Charles watched her go, with no regret, and turned to the vicar.

"Please do continue – we have a wedding to complete!"

A short while later, to the enthusiastic applause of the guests, Charles kissed Catherine again, as his wife, and swept her up to carry her towards the door, leaning in to whisper "Thaddeus awaits, my Countess."

She giggled uncontrollably as he threw the church doors open.

They passed on out into the world, free and in love, with the sound of an entire church's rapturous applause ringing in their ears.

# The End

AR
Arietta Richmond
Regency Historical Romance

Arietta Richmond has been a compulsive reader and writer all her life. Whilst her reading has covered an enormous range of topics, history has always fascinated her, and historical novels have been amongst her favourite reading.

She has written a wide range of work, from business articles and other non-fiction works (published under a pen name) but fiction has always been a major part of her life. Now, her Regency Historical Romance books are finally being released. The Derbyshire Set is comprised of 11 novels (9 released so far). The 'His Majesty's Hounds' series is comprised of 17 novels, with the last now released.

She also has a number of standalone novels released, and four other series of novels at various stages of release. She lives in Australia, and when not reading or writing, likes to travel, and to see in person the places where history happened.

Be the first to know about it when Arietta's next book is released! Sign up to Arietta's newsletter at

http://www.ariettarichmond.com

When you do, you will receive two free subscriber exclusive books - **'A Gift of Love',** which is a prequel to the Derbyshire Set series, and ends on the day that 'The Earl's Unexpected Bride' begins, and **'Madame's Christmas Marquis'** which is an additional story in the His Majesty's Hounds series.

These stories are not for sale anywhere – they are absolutely exclusive to newsletter subscribers!

# Connect with Arietta:

Donate and support her on Kofi.com
https://ko-fi.com/ariettarichmondauthor

Follow her on Amazon - https://www.amazon.com/Arietta-Richmond/e/B016GG1KJ6/

Like her Facebook Page - https://www.facebook.com/AriettaRichmondAuthor

Follow her on Twitter - https://twitter.com/AriettaRichmond

Follow her on Instagram - https://www.instagram.com/AriettaRichmond/

Follow her on Bookbub – https://www.bookbub.com/authors/arietta-richmond

Follow her on Goodreads - https://www.goodreads.com/author/show/14508806.Arietta Richmond

Here is your preview of the next book in

'The Derbyshire Set':

## "The Captain's Compromised Heiress"

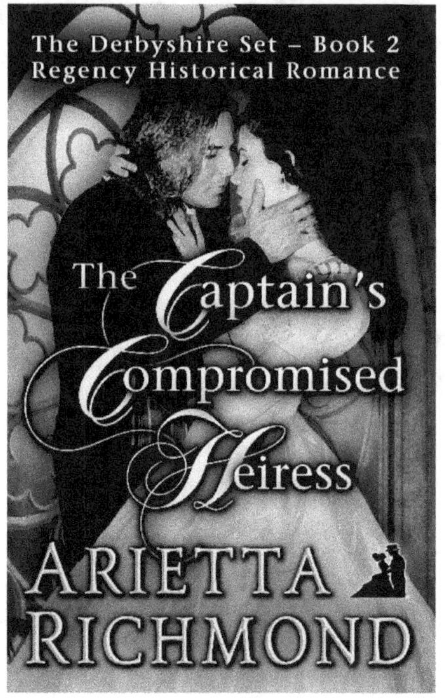

**ARIETTA RICHMOND**

The moment that Blanchette saw Captain Westbury's uniform, she knew that this party had not been a mistake. For days now she had argued with her mother and sister, insisting that it was all too soon, too close to the nightmare that had been her aborted wedding to the Earl of Stanningfield, for her to be able to cope with society once again.

They had recited the same old arguments; she needed to move ahead in her life, she couldn't go on moping and crying, over having been jilted at the altar, for ever more. The incident may have stirred up a scandal in Derbyshire society and beyond, but she was still one of the most desirable young ladies in England, with a substantial portion as well, and would surely find a suitable match soon enough. She had dismissed all of their reasoning and sulked, but, in that instant of her first sight of Captain Westbury, with her heart pitter-pattering like a cantering mare, all that could be put aside.

Hope, romance, and desire all rose suddenly within her, fresh sensations once again.

"Captain Henry Westbury of the Coldstream Guards, heir to The Most Honourable Sir Thomas Westbury, Marquess of Bevington."

The footman, in his sumptuous livery, made the announcement over the sound of the room's chatter, and it took an immense effort for all of the ladies present to maintain their calm demeanour and resist the urge to turn, as one, and stare at this new arrival.

His rank and title spoke for him - a soldier, so gallant and well-attired, and also with a claim to one of the great estates in England. Such a man would be a desirable husband for any daughter of a noble family, and all present were immediately aware of that fact.

Not only this however, but from the perspective of a young lady, with ideas about romance learned from novels and whispered gossip between sisters, this Captain Westbury was an exceptionally handsome gentleman.

His golden hair sat thick and lush upon his head, immaculately curled, matching the colour of his shining brass buttons.

The military stock and collar, in the dark facings of his most esteemed regiment of guardsmen, seemed almost to frame his face like a painting, and perfectly emphasised the delicate curvature of his bone structure, slender and pleasing.

There was serenity in his blue eyes that nevertheless, when matched with his glorious mane and shimmering scarlet uniform seemed to give him an inner strength that radiated outwards.

He was tall and well-proportioned, with long-legs clad in skin-tight buff breeches and high leather boots, designed for the parade ground and polished to a glinting sheen. His entire manner and bearing was confident, even heroic, and he strode out into the room with every female eye fixed discreetly, or not so discreetly, upon him.

Blanchette suppressed an urge to laugh. Could it really have been only a few hours ago that she had been sitting in the library of this very house, her house, here on the edge of Amfield Moor, morosely carrying on a conversation with her sister Charlotte about her desire to run away and be done with men and society for good?

"Oh Blanche, you must not talk such rubbish!" Charlotte had declared back confidently.

"Why just because one eligible bachelor has spurned you does not mean that they all will! What happened in Suffolk was a freak, a bizarre little incident that historians will look at a hundred years from now and declare to be one of the strangest occurrences in the annals of the English gentry! You were just unlucky that's all".

"But Charlotte…" Blanche had replied, trying with all her might not to burst into tears once again. "…what if it's me? What if there is something about me, which Stanningfield, Charles, found profoundly unattractive? What if it's all somehow my problem and men don't take to me?"

"My dear Blanche, I am not sure what that is even supposed to mean. Why, you're pretty, you're clever, you're from an exceptionally good family, if I do say so myself. Don't talk rubbish! If you are to declare that you have certain deficiencies of appearance or character that make you unattractive, what possible hope is there for me?"

They had shared a little laugh at this. It had always been known to both of them that Blanche was, as the eldest and the prettier of the pair, the one who would be first to find a husband. She secretly suspected that Charlotte resented her for this fact, but her sister was kind and knowing enough not to let on. The truth was that Blanche's failed marriage put Charlotte in a very awkward position. It was unlikely that a betrothal would be sought, or agree if proposed for he, until her older sister was herself wed.

Indeed, in her worst moments, Charlotte did wonder if, as the youngest, there was a chance that her family might decide they would rather not be parted from her ever, if she did not have the chance to seek a husband soon. An unsaid tension was growing between the two sisters, despite Charlotte's willingness to try and stem her sisters' tears.

"Here is my personal guarantee," Charlotte had declared, smiling. "If you don't have attractive and suitable gentlemen positively queueing up to ask you to dance with them at the ball tonight, why then I'll personally ride naked through the streets of Chesterfield. You have that as a guarantee, signed by my own hand and sealed with the Cavendish family crest!"

Blanche was rather shocked by that image, but had laughed, nonetheless. They had shaken hands in a comical imitation of City gentlemen, and embraced. The truth from Blanche's perspective was that she had never doubted Charlotte's prospects of finding a man. She could be very funny and was shamelessly flirtatious, and their mother had never suggested keeping either of them unwed.

Perhaps the younger of the Cavendish sisters knew that having a moping spinster ahead of her in the marriage queue was no good to anyone.

Whatever her motives, Blanche was glad of the kindness. Now that Captain Westbury had made his appearance she was more than glad.

In fact, she was positively delighted that her mother had decided to host this house party, and ball (the fact that it allowed her mother to indulge in her penchant for bringing together unwed persons of distinction was a side benefit, from Blanche's point of view), and that so many had decided to come. None had yet raised the subject of her unfortunate jilting at the hands of Charles Rockingham, Earl of Stanningfield, many of whom present privately knew to be an eccentric and impulsive sort of a man in any case.

For a while she had sat at the back of the room gathering her courage and resolve, sipping at a glass of ratafia, while Charlotte batted her eyelashes and laughed at the men's jokes, but now she pressed forward, concealing half of her beautiful heart shaped face with a fan, and casting what she hoped were dark and mysterious looks with her piercing gaze.

She could see immediately that Captain Westbury, who was still by the door exchanging pleasantries with his hosts, her mother and father, had noticed her.

She was not in the least surprised when he ignored several of the ladies nearer the entrance, blushing and fiddling with their hair, and made straight for her. The newfound sense of confidence, that this created, carried her into their conversation with a strong sense of her attractiveness, and of the ample possibilities this evening, and the rest of this week, afforded.

"Lady Blanchette, I assume?" he asked wryly, bending to kiss her hand in a single, practised motion.

Her heart fluttered and she felt something new stirring in her, low in her body. It was a sensation she was quite unused to, a trembling and a warmth. She had felt desire before, had felt nervous, had felt many things, but never exactly this.

It startled her, but, if pressed, she would not have said that it was an unpleasant sensation. She looked at Captain Westbury's clean-cut jawline, and felt his firm hand around hers and the sensation came on all the stronger.

"You presume correctly, Captain Westbury," she replied, barely making eye contact. She could see that Charlotte, on the other side of the room, had noticed and was now watching, distracted, no longer all that interested in the red-haired fellow she had been flirting with. "Tell me, what brings a soldier of the esteemed Coldstream Guards to our humble occasion at Amfield?"

"Why, the same things that attract anyone to an occasion such as this - the promise of society with one's peers, of hunting, and the prospect of meeting, and conversing with, attractive young ladies."

"And I trust your hopes in that regard have not been disappointed?"

"Certainly not," - he had a direct and bluff manner of speaking that she suspected he had learned in the military. "I had heard about his Lordship's fair young daughters and assumed that reports of their grace and beauty had been exaggerated. But now that I am able to make a reconnaissance with my own eyes, I can see that they were quite understated in their praise".

"You think so? And may I hope that it is not daughters in the plural that you are here to make an aesthetic appraisal of?"

For the first time she allowed herself to make full eye contact with him.

Their eyes met, two pools of intense blue, each hinting at fascinating hidden depths.

He seemed momentarily taken off guard by her quip, and her heart picked up its pace once again, at precisely the same moment that the string quartet on the far side of the room increased their tempo.

Was it the music, she thought for a second, that was making her feel like this, or the company?

"I shall have to see," he responded coolly. "After all, it would be ill-mannered of me not to make the effort of acquainting myself with all of the young ladies present, would it not?"

"I suppose that depends on your perspective," she said back, with a flutter of her fan.

"Nevertheless," he said, regaining some composure, "I was considering asking you to dance with me at once, and I would consider it most disappointing if you were to refuse. May I dare to hope that there may be a space on your dance card – for this very dance?"

Blanche made show of consulting her dance card carefully, even though she knew exactly what was written on there – which was, due to her hiding in the shadows earlier, precisely nothing.

She looked up, and was immediately caught again by his deep blue eyes.

"Would you be so very disappointed Captain? I suppose in that case, I should feel duty-bound to accept."

With an intriguing smile, that promised much but gave away almost nothing, she placed her hand daintily on his offered arm, and allowed him to take her off to the centre of the room to dance.

154

Continued...

Read the rest at :

https://ariettarichmond.com/go/the-captains-compromised-heiress

Get

# "The Captain's Compromised Heiress"

And the rest of the series now!

Make sure that you are the first to see news and new book release notices!

Sign up now at:

http://www.ariettarichmond.com

when you do, you will also get the

**free, subscriber exclusive prequel story**
**'A Gift of Love'**

– <u>not available anywhere else</u> – your chance to find out more about Theodora, and what happened before the start of The Earl's Unexpected Bride!

## Books in The Derbyshire Set

The Earl's Unexpected Bride

The Captain's Compromised Heiress

The Viscount's Unsuitable Affair

The Count's Impetuous Seduction

The Rake's Unlikely Redemption

The Marquess' Scandalous Mistress

The Marchioness' Second Chance

A Viscount's Reluctant Passion

Lady Theodora's Christmas Wish

The Derbyshire Set Omnibus Edition Vol. 1 (the first three books all in one)

The Derbyshire Set Omnibus Edition Vol. 2 (the second three books all in one)

The Derbyshire Set Omnibus Edition Vol. 3 (the third three books all in one)

# Books in the His Majesty's Hounds Series

Claiming the Heart of a Duke

Intriguing the Viscount

Giving a Heart of Lace

Being Lady Harriet's Hero

Enchanting the Duke

Redeeming the Marquess

Finding the Duke's Heir

Winning the Merchant Earl

Healing Lord Barton

Kissing the Duke of Hearts

Loving the Bitter Baron

Falling for the Earl

Rescuing the Countess

Betting on a Lady's Heart

Attracting the Spymaster

Courting a Spinster for Christmas

Restoring the Earl's Honour

From Soldier Spy to Lord (Books 1 to 3 as a set)

To Love a Determined Lady (Books 4 to 6 as a set)

Love Heals a Lord (Books 7 to 9 as a set)

To Love a Dashing Lord (Books 10 to 13 as a set)

For a Lady's Honour (Books 14 to 17 as a set)

The Barrington Saga (all books related to the Barrington Family)

# Books in the A Duke's Daughters – the Elbury Bouquet Series

## Books in the Regency Scandals Series

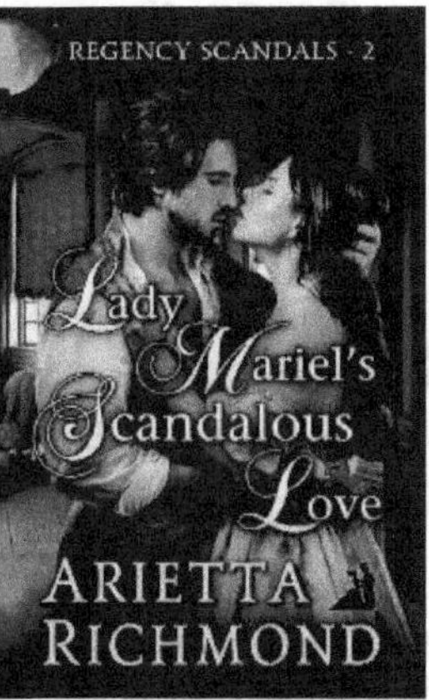

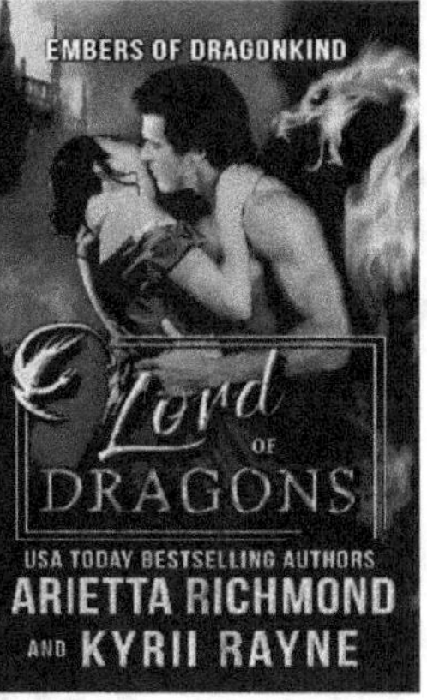

# Books in the Nettlefold Chronicles

## Books in the Regency Gothic Series

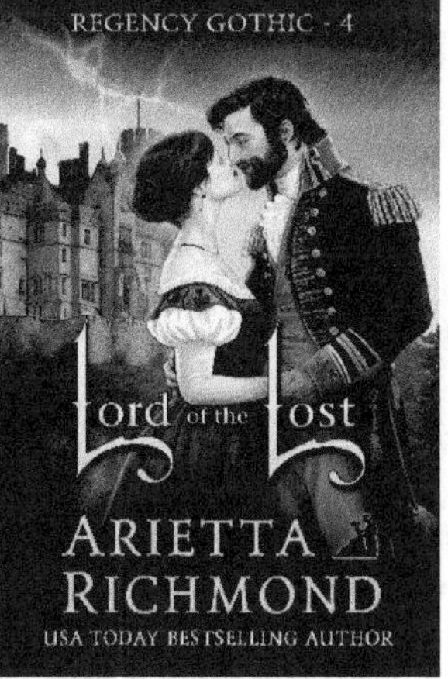

# Regency Collections with Other Authors

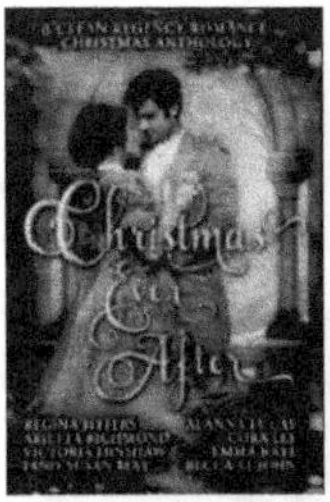
Christmas Ever After
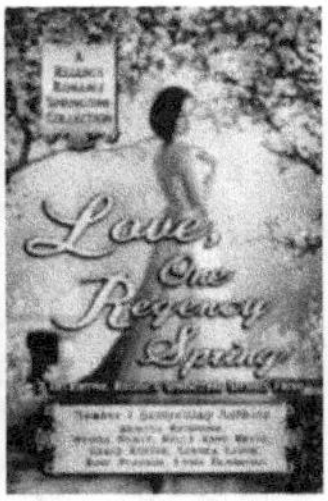
Love, One Regency Spring
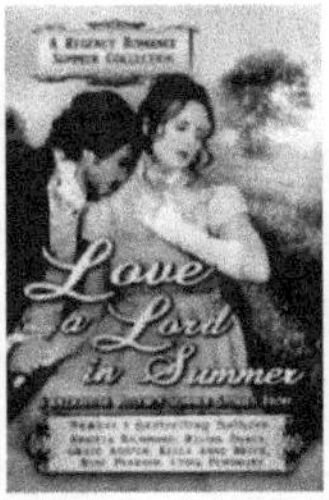
A Regency Romance Summer Collection
Love for a Lord in Summer
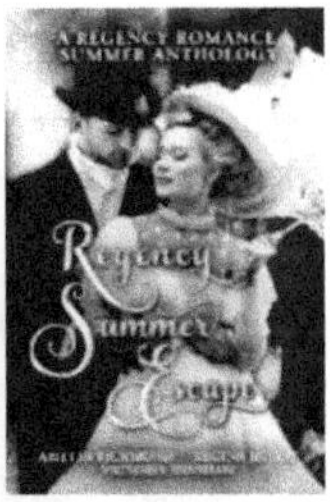
A REGENCY ROMANCE SUMMER ANTHOLOGY
Regency Summer Escapes

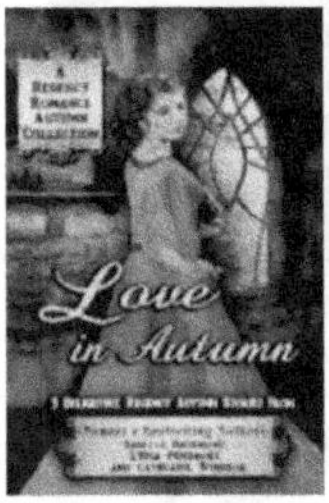
Love in Autumn
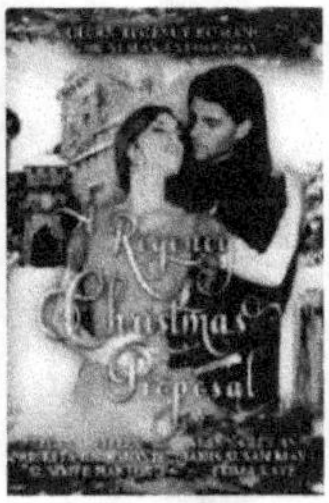
A Regency Christmas Proposal
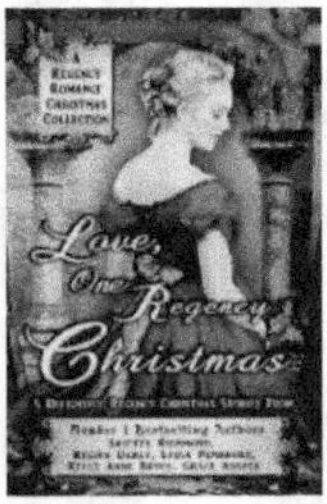
Love, One Regency Christmas
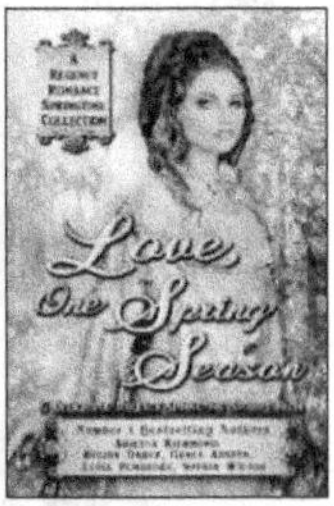
Love, One Spring Season

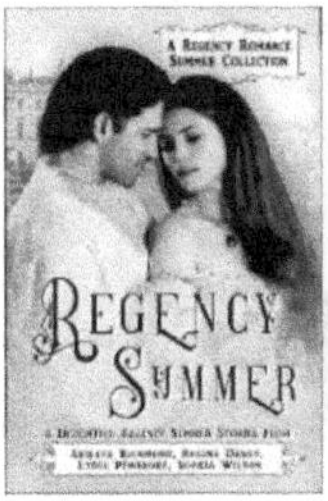
A Regency Romance Summer Collection
REGENCY SUMMER
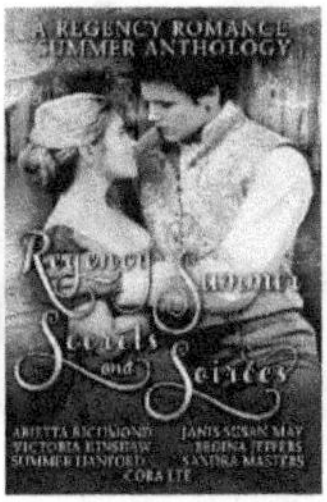
A REGENCY ROMANCE SUMMER ANTHOLOGY
Regency Summer Secrets and Soirées
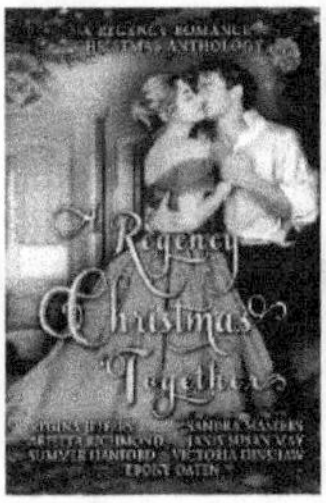
A Regency Christmas Together
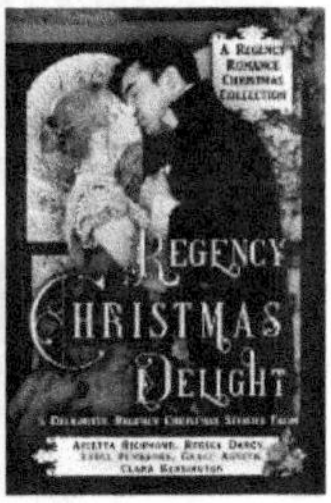
A Regency Romance Christmas Collection
REGENCY CHRISTMAS DELIGHT

A REGENCY ROMANCE SUMMER ANTHOLOGY
Regency Mid-Summer Mischief
A REGENCY ROMANCE CHRISTMAS ANTHOLOGY
Regency Missives and Mischief
A REGENCY ROMANCE SUMMER ANTHOLOGY
Regency Summer Garden
A REGENCY ROMANCE CHRISTMAS ANTHOLOGY
A Regency Christmas Doubled

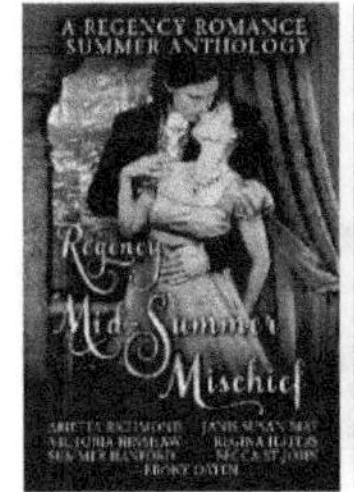

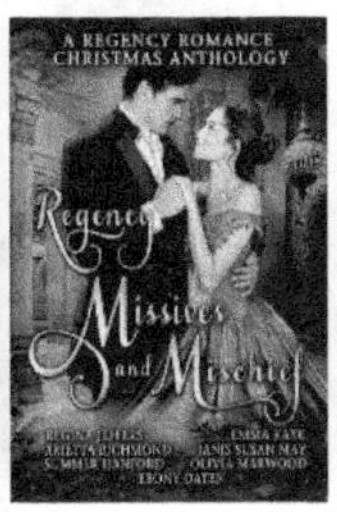

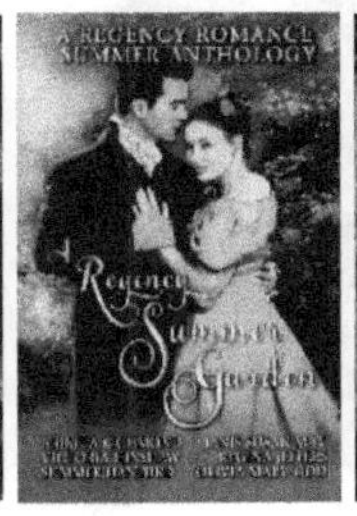

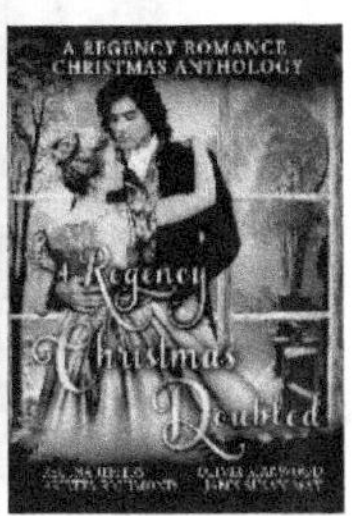

# Themed Regency Collections

*The Her Duke Collection*

## Other Books from Arietta

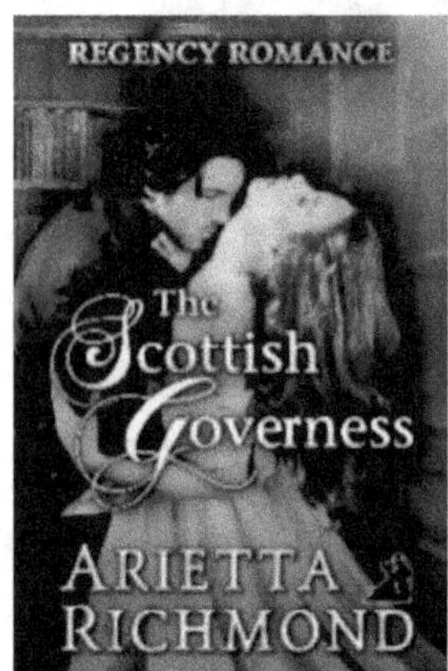

# Other Books from Dreamstone Publishing

Dreamstone publishes books in a wide variety of categories – here are some of our other bestselling books:-

We have books in many categories, ranging from Erotica and Romance to Kids Books, Business Books, Photography, Cook Books, Diaries, Colouring books and much more. New books released each month.

Be the first to know when our next books are coming out

Be first to get all the news – sign up for our newsletter at

http://www.dreamstonepublishing.com

www.ingramcontent.com/pod-product-compliance
Lightning Source LLC
Chambersburg PA
CBHW070957180726
48291CB00004B/1340